Nothing c   that they were both all right from showing on her face.

Adam must have seen it, because he grinned.

"See, I knew you still cared. At least a little," he teased.

He was lucky she didn't want the hassle of an internal affairs investigation—because she wanted nothing more than to slap that grin off of his face.

"You don't get how serious this is, do you?" Shiloh muttered between clenched teeth. She scanned the area, unable to suppress a shiver. Gut instinct said someone was out there. Watching.

"I get it." Adam's voice sobered. "I know that someone tried..." His voice trailed off.

"Tried to kill us," she finished for him.

Frustration and fear fought for dominance. Shiloh took a few deep breaths, tried to stay calm, but finally could hold back no longer. She kicked the side of the car. When she considered the incident with the snake that morning, she knew the two events had to be connected. And that could only mean one thing.

They'd found her.

SARAH VARLAND

lives in the woods in Georgia with her husband, John, their two boys and their dogs. Her passion for books comes from her mom, and her love for suspense comes from her dad who has spent a career in law enforcement. Her love for romance comes from the relationship she has with her husband and from watching too many chick flicks. When she's not writing, she's often found reading, baking, kayaking or hiking.

TREASURE POINT SECRETS

SARAH VARLAND

HARLEQUIN® LOVE INSPIRED® SUSPENSE

Recycling programs
for this product may
not exist in your area.

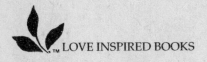

TM LOVE INSPIRED BOOKS

ISBN-13: 978-0-373-44599-8

TREASURE POINT SECRETS

www.Harlequin.com

Printed in U.S.A.

The Lord your God is in your midst,
a mighty one who will save;
He will rejoice over you with gladness;
He will quiet you by His love;
He will exult over you with loud singing.
—*Zephaniah* 3:17

Dedication

To my family. You encourage me, love me and
let me talk about made-up people like they're real.
I couldn't ask for more.

Acknowledgments

Thank you, John, for the endless pages you read
and edited. Most of all, thank you for
being a better man than any hero I could make up—
you teach me what love is every day.

Thanks to Joshua and Timothy, for letting me
go in my "working bubble" sometimes.

Thanks, Mom and Dad, for coming to so many
conferences with me. Mom, thanks for the
babysitting marathons so I could get this book
written. Dad, thanks for answering endless
questions about all things law enforcement.

Thanks to Alison, for teasing me
about never finishing a story.

Thanks to my friends who have encouraged
and critiqued along the way.

Thanks to my editor, Elizabeth, for knowing exactly
how to polish this story and for all the work
you put into making it the best it could be.

And thank you, Lord, for the chance to do this.
I pray you're glorified.

PROLOGUE

Shiloh Evans stood alone in the empty church grave-yard, surveying the freshly packed earth in front of the hard granite stone, knowing there were three fresh graves nearly identical to it in several other Savannah cemeteries. A breeze—too warm—rustled the branches of a live-oak tree, creaking its limbs in an eerie melody. It would storm before the day was done.

Though she hated storms—had since she was a little girl—it wasn't that threat on the horizon that sent goose bumps up her bare arms and made her shiver in the August air.

There were four graves, not five. She guessed Providence had seen to that for now. She stood motionless, unable to take her eyes from the stark headstone. There was something haunting in knowing she wasn't supposed to be alive.

Four graves.

If they ever found her, there would be five. She forced her gaze away from the cemetery and took purposeful steps toward her car.

She felt the subtle shift in the air less than a second before she heard the sizzle and pop of a lightning bolt striking close by.

Too close.

She got in her car, and then Shiloh looked back. She watched in her rearview mirror as the skies opened up, pouring rain on the fresh earth.

She had to leave, but she wasn't running. She was regrouping. Preparing. One day she'd have the opportunity to bring the killers to justice, to see the criminals pay for what they had done. In the meantime, they would look for her, eventually come after her.

And Shiloh would be ready.

ONE

Five Years Later...

Shiloh rolled down the windows of her police cruiser and took a deep breath of the humid air. It was times like this—with the scenery in front of her and the faint taste of salt from the ocean on the breeze—that she missed Savannah. Something about the graceful, beautiful, dangerous city tugged at her and begged her to return, but Shiloh knew she never could.

The light dimmed even further, taking the area from gold to gray, and Shiloh shivered. She knew it was only from the sun dipping behind a cloud. That had nothing to do with her thoughts about Savannah. The timing was coincidence.

Nevertheless she glanced around, suddenly overtaken by an uneasy feeling she was being watched. That the past had finally found her, as she'd always known it would.

She saw nothing. But she rolled up the windows anyway. Better safe than sorry. Or dead.

She hated feeling afraid after all these years, even after being proactive to combat the fear. She'd become a police officer partially so she could be on the offensive—someone who was working to bring justice to the men who had wreaked havoc on her family's lives five years ago—instead of a victim.

At times like this, she felt as if she'd failed. She stole a glance at the sky, wishing God would listen if she asked for His help to overcome this fear. But she'd stopped expecting Him to listen five years ago.

Instead, she focused on the road as the old plantation-style house she'd been assigned to check out came into view. Shiloh knew it must have been white once, but it was dulled now to a phantom gray. It seemed to lean on the columns that had once made the front porch regal and graceful, but now served only to keep the house from falling under the weight it carried. She couldn't help but feel, if the house could talk, it would be able to explain its weary appearance.

As she parked her car and opened her door, Shiloh tried to shake off the melancholy that had overtaken her. The past had stayed where it belonged for five long, empty years. There was no reason to believe that would change today.

She focused on the reason she was here. Widow Hamilton called the police department two or three times a week with concerns. The reason changed, but her calls were consistent. It was a common assumption the motive behind the calls was loneliness.

She wished it was an option to send the police chaplain out to see the widow and offer her some company. Generally, chaplains did more work with the officers themselves, but Widow Hamilton and her paranoia were making it difficult for everyone in the department.

Unfortunately, they didn't have a chaplain at the moment. The former chaplain had worked at the Treasure Point Police Department—probably since Treasure Point was founded back in 1734—until his family had finally convinced him to retire. Shiloh didn't envy whoever tried to take his place. The former chaplain had left enormous shoes to fill, and the people of Treasure Point—while loving and protective of their own—weren't the easiest group to break into. The new chaplain, whoever he was, would have his work cut out for him.

Shiloh knocked on the front door, taking a deep breath to steel herself against whatever problems the widow thought she was having today.

"Mrs. Hamilton? It's Shiloh Evans, from the Treasure Point Police Department. Mrs. Hamilton, are you there? Can you hear me?"

No one answered. Shiloh glanced to the detached garage on the right, to see if there was a car inside, but the door was down. More than likely the woman was out running errands around town. Shiloh was tempted to simply turn around and leave. But even though she was relatively certain there was nothing to the widow's fears, Mrs. Hamilton counted on the police department to take her concerns seriously. With that in mind, Shiloh walked around the side of the house, noting that if the widow was truly concerned about intruders, she'd take care of the overgrown bushes, which would make an ideal hiding place for someone who was up to no good.

"If anyone's there, come out now. Don't make me come in after you." There was only silence—not a single rustle. The quiet should have been comforting. It wasn't. Instead, it added to the tense, charged feeling running up and down her spine. She glared at the bushes as she walked by, narrowing her eyes to make absolutely sure no one was hiding in them. She saw nothing, only the dense green leaves. Still she shivered.

"Keep it together, Evans. You don't want to have to explain that you discharged your weapon because you got spooked by some shrubbery."

When she reached the back of the house, she knocked on the back door. No answer there, either. She peeked in several windows and noted that nothing looked out of place or disturbed. Duty done, Shiloh walked back to her car, eager to continue with her day. And maybe find some decent coffee to make up for the morning she'd had so far.

Shiloh got in her car and was reaching up to turn the key when movement near the passenger seat caught her eye.

She froze and turned her gaze in the direction of whatever had moved. The first thing she noticed was an unfamiliar burlap sack on the floorboard.

The second was the coiled-up form of what looked like a timber rattlesnake.

Her heart pounded as she reached to slowly open her door. She managed to get it almost all the way open without the snake noticing, but the final push caught the rattler's attention and startled it.

The snake tensed.

So did Shiloh. She sat there, skin crawling at being inches away from the viper, not knowing if moving would startle it into striking. They sat for several long seconds, Shiloh caught in indecision over what to do until a soft rattle made up her mind.

Not caring where she landed, Shiloh threw herself backward, squeezing her eyes shut and praying she'd be fast enough to make it out before the snake struck.

She hit the ground hard enough to knock the wind out of her, but she kept her head enough to kick the door shut behind her. She stood up, backed warily away from her car and the dangerous reptile, and reached for her radio.

"Unit 807 to dispatch—" Shiloh took a deep breath "—there's a poisonous snake in my vehicle."

She didn't have to wait long for a reply. After a crackle

of static, she heard "Unit 807, this is dispatch. We have a car coming your way."

Relief came and then dissipated like liquid on a hot summer day as what had happened fully sank in. The burlap sack on the floor of the car said that snake hadn't ended up there by accident.

Someone was trying to kill her.

Shiloh's car had been de-snaked and examined for evidence, and she'd been cleared for duty. She took a deep breath, trying to relieve the tension that had built as she'd sat by helplessly while other officers investigated the car for evidence—as if there was any she might have missed. Then she'd had to convince the chief that she was fine and more than capable of finishing her shift. Treasure Point was a quiet little town, but that didn't mean that law enforcement could afford to just take the day off. The town had its share of troublemakers.

Like the driver of the truck in front of her that had been practically flying down the road but was now parked on the shoulder. She didn't recognize the vehicle, but anyone going sixty in a 35 mph zone was showing blatant disrespect for the law.

She opened her door and approached the driver's side of the pickup. She reached the window and saw that the man inside was...

Talking on a *cell phone?*

Shiloh mentally counted to ten. Talking on a cell phone *while* you were being pulled over?

Shiloh shook her head and tapped lightly on the glass.

He waved her off.

She tapped again. Harder.

This time he held up his index finger—the universal *one second* sign.

One second? Oh, sure, she had the time to wait. It wasn't as if she had areas to patrol, crimes to solve...

Shiloh scanned the area. She didn't see anything out of the ordinary, but the prickly feeling on the back of her neck refused to go away.

She was reaching to tap on the glass—for the *third* time— when the stranger rolled down his window.

"Sorry about that."

The too-familiar voice registered in her mind a split second before the mossy-green eyes locked with hers.

This man was no stranger.

"Adam?"

Adam's heart was still pounding from the conversation he'd been having. The former congregation member's depression had been so striking that it had taken Adam's attention off his speedometer. When he'd noticed the lights and sirens behind him, he'd ended the call, leaving her with strict instructions to phone the senior pastor of the church. While pulling over, he'd then called the pastor to brief him on the situation so he could handle it from there.

Guilt had been his primary reaction when he'd realized he'd been speeding. But that feeling, along with every emotion other than shock, vanished as he looked straight into the face of the most gorgeous cop—scratch that—the most gorgeous *woman* he'd ever seen. Still, even after all these years.

"Shiloh." Memories rushed through him as he said her name out loud. Memories of her laughing, the two of them running together on Tybee Island, racing into the ocean at the end. The feeling of her lips on his.

"Do you know how fast you were going?"

She practically spat the words through gritted teeth. Apparently, seeing him didn't bring back the same set of pleasant memories for her. He thought of their last few weeks together, before she'd left town five years ago: the death of her cousin, Annie; Shiloh's declared intent to someday find the killer; their disagreement over his dad's—her pastor's—stance on women in law enforcement.

Okay, if those were the things she was thinking about, it was no wonder she looked so mad.

"I don't," he answered honestly. All he knew was that it had been too fast. "About the cell phone..."

She had already pulled out her notebook and was jotting things down, but she looked up to level him with a glare. "Important call?"

He didn't miss the sarcasm lacing her tone. "Look, Shiloh..."

"Officer Evans."

Really? She *was* mad.

"Officer Evans." He forced the words out even though they seemed awfully formal for the woman he'd been planning to marry five years ago. "The phone call honestly was an emergency. Someone was contemplating suicide, and I was afraid to hang up abruptly. And once I did end the call, I needed to phone someone nearby to put him in touch with her. I am sorry."

Her eyes flicked up from her notepad, and she gave a slight nod, though her taut facial muscles didn't relax.

"License and registration, please?"

He handed her both and waited as she took down the information, then checked the rear of the car to write down his plate numbers and walked back to him. She handed him the yellow ticket along with his documentation. "Here you go." Shiloh turned to her cruiser, not giving him a second glance.

"That's it?" Adam called out the window. "Not going to

say hi, fill me in on what you've been up to for five years? Ask why I'm in town?"

The eyes she turned on him flashed fire. And, yeah, he'd provoked her deliberately, but it got to him that seeing him didn't affect her at all.

"Fine. Hi, Adam." She stumbled over his name, as though it hurt her to say it. "I'm a police officer now. What are you doing here?"

"Nice to see you, too," he said calmly. "A police officer, huh? I'm the new pastor for Creekview Church."

"Like father, like son, right?" She shook her head. "Guess I'm not surprised. Welcome to Treasure Point."

Funny, she sounded slightly less than welcoming.

He reached to roll up his window as she walked away, until he caught the words she tossed over her shoulder.

"By the way, your rear left tire is flat. Must've run over a nail."

It figured. He had been so caught up in his conversation that he hadn't noticed. He squeezed his eyes shut, running over his options. He was now more than fifteen minutes late to his meeting. There was no way he had time to change a tire first.

He was stuck. And Shiloh—*Officer Evans*—was his only option.

He pushed open the truck door, walked to her car and tapped on her window.

She jammed her finger down on the button and glared up at him when the window was fully open. "What?"

Adam smiled what he hoped was his most charming smile. "Any chance you could give me a ride?"

She flung her door wide, narrowly missing hitting him in the leg.

He raised his hands in mock surrender. "You don't have to get upset. I won't be any trouble. And I can let myself in." He headed toward the passenger side until the sound of Shiloh snickering stopped him.

"What?"

She reached for the rear door of the patrol car, opened it and motioned to the backseat. "You can ride here."

"You've got to be kidding."

She only raised her eyebrows. "Did you want a ride or not?"

Adam climbed in, thankful that he'd left his dog with a friend in Savannah and made plans to pick him up and bring him to town along with the rest of his belongings in the next day or two. He couldn't imagine how well it would have gone over if he'd had to ask for a ride for both him and the dog, especially since he seemed to rank somewhere near the bottom of Shiloh's "favorite person" list.

He tried not to think about where he was sitting as he took in the scenery, observing the town through the windows.

It looked like every other small town he'd been in along Georgia's coast, but it appeared to be a nice place to live. Anticipation coursed through his veins—hopefully, it would be a good place for his first solo pastoring job. His dad's connections had found the job for him, and Adam wanted to do his best work here—make sure he didn't let God, or his dad, down. He wasn't sure which possibility scared him more.

He looked at Shiloh and noticed she was checking the rearview mirror every few seconds. The tense set of her jaw made it clear that something was wrong. Something more than having her ex-fiancé in the backseat of her cruiser.

Adam looked over his shoulder. An older-model gray sedan was following them.

He glanced at Shiloh, still staring in the rearview, so he turned his head again. The car behind them inched closer.

Shiloh sped up.

So did the other car.

Adam turned to the front again, watching Shiloh's face through the clear barrier. Her jaw was set, but there was a glimmer of fear in her eyes.

"Shiloh, what's going on?"

She didn't answer.

He looked up the road ahead of them. If they made it across that bridge, then they'd be in town.

"Do you think they'll back off once we're in town and there are people around?"

"I don't know." The dread he heard in her tone settled deep in his own gut.

A car in the approaching lane sped toward them. Adam tensed. Not likely that was a coincidence.

The bridge loomed closer. They were twenty, maybe thirty, yards away when the car coming at them swerved deliberately into their lane.

Understanding slammed into Adam, made him work to catch his breath.

They were trying to force them into a collision. Were they after Shiloh? And why?

He didn't have time to ask more questions or to figure out anything else. They'd reached critical mass. Adam braced himself for impact, thankful that he was spiritually ready to die—even if he'd have rather put it off for a while—and closed his eyes. Visions of fiery car crashes he'd seen during his chaplain training haunted him. He didn't want that to be his final thought.

So he opened his eyes, took one more look at Shiloh.

Instead of looking resigned, she appeared ready for a fight. Adam's eyes widened as he realized what she was doing.

Shiloh yanked the wheel hard right, and the car clipped

the guardrail with their left front side as she avoided the bridge and careened straight toward the last place Adam would have thought would be a good idea.

Straight into Hamilton Creek.

TWO

Shiloh fought the urge to close her eyes and instead fixated on steering the car straight into the creek.

The car slammed into the water, arresting their speed to something approaching slow motion. Water sloshed and caught the vehicle, bringing them to a stop in the middle of the creek.

She released her breath as she looked out the window. Would have uttered a prayer of thanks if she had thought God was paying attention.

Shiloh pushed at the door, but it wouldn't budge. With about three feet of standing water, the pressure was too great.

Water trickled in through the cracks in the doors. Shiloh's chest tightened, and she fought to breathe even though there was still plenty of fresh air in the car.

No. She couldn't let fear overtake her and she refused to sit here while the cruiser filled with water. She had to use her head, use her training and stay focused on the situation. She looked around for something to use to break the window, eyes catching immediately on her black baton on the passenger-side floorboard. She reached for it, tensing as she remembered the snake that had been there not two hours before.

Shiloh tightened her grip on the stick and smashed it through the window.

She pulled her body through the opening, careful not to catch herself on any of the remaining jagged glass, and stood in the midthigh water as movement in the back of the car caught her eye.

Adam.

For a minute, in her panic, she'd forgotten he was there.

Shiloh glanced down at the door handle but knew trying to pull it open would be futile. She couldn't break the glass for him with her baton without shattering it all over him and risking an injury. She might not *like* him, but she'd never hurt him on purpose.

"Move!" he yelled through the window and motioned with his hand for her to back away.

She stepped aside and watched as he brought his arm back and smashed something—a pocketknife, maybe—through the window. It took a few more seconds for him to clear enough glass to get through, then he climbed out as she had and joined her in the murky water.

Nothing could have kept the relief she felt from showing on her face. Adam must have seen it, because he grinned.

"See, I knew you still cared. At least a little," he teased.

He was lucky she didn't want the hassle of an internal-affairs investigation—because she wanted nothing more than to slap that grin off his face.

"You don't get how serious this is, do you?" Shiloh muttered between clenched teeth. She scanned the marshy area around the creek again, unable to suppress a shiver as she did so. Next her gaze landed at the creek's banks, which would make ideal cover for a sniper. Nothing—that she saw.

But her gut instinct, which had served her well before, said someone was out here. Watching.

"I get it." Adam's voice had sobered. "I mean, I don't. It

makes no sense. But, yeah, I know that someone tried..." His voice trailed off.

"Tried to kill us," she finished for him, then swallowed hard and focused her attention on the bridge. No cars. Her pursuer and his accomplice were long gone, and she had no leads—not a license-plate number and no worthwhile description, since almost every car involved in a crime was a "dark midsize sedan."

Frustration and fear fought for dominance. Shiloh tried to stay calm but finally could hold back no longer. She kicked the side of the car, doing nothing more than splashing muddy salt water all over herself. When she considered the incident with the snake that morning, she knew the two events had to be connected. And that could mean only one thing.

They'd found her.

She'd known it wouldn't be hard for them. She had moved only an hour away, to this small town, which seemed like the perfect haven. Though she'd left Savannah five years ago—determined to do her best to solve the case and be ready for the criminals once they came after her—she hadn't expected the past to find her *today*.

Maybe she wasn't as prepared as she'd thought.

But until now it had been quiet. Probably too quiet. She'd almost started to hope that they had realized she didn't have whatever they were looking for, and that she could wrap this up and bring them to justice without becoming a target again. Shiloh studied the too-quiet landscape, finally settling on the question that weighed heavily on her mind.

Why now?

Shiloh shook her head, scanned their surroundings again and concluded that finding the answer would have to wait until she wasn't standing out in the open—not to mention nearly up to her waist—in dirty, smelly water. She radioed the station, gave their location and a short description of what had happened, as she slogged through the water to the shore.

"Shiloh?"

She jumped at his voice and relaxed as her mind registered that it was only Adam, who'd joined her on the creek's bank.

Only Adam… She turned toward him and narrowed her eyes. "How is it that you show up in town and suddenly someone wants me dead?"

He jerked back as if she had slapped him. "What?"

"I've been attacked twice today—the same day I see you for the first time in five years. This seems entirely too coincidental to me."

"Let's back up. You think someone's trying to kill you because I came to town?"

Everything about the expression on his face said it wasn't true. Her heart simultaneously sank and danced. It sank because if he didn't know why his arrival would have put her in danger, then she was back to square one. Shiloh didn't want to think about why it danced. Other than to admit that, heartbreaker or not, Adam had always been someone she had trusted. One of the only people alive. She wanted to believe he was still worthy of that trust.

"I'd never let anyone hurt you. You know that."

He touched her arm lightly and even pressing thoughts, like the danger she was in, left her for a split second.

She had to resist this chemistry. Trust was one thing. Falling for him again was another. She and Adam were wrong for each other in every way that mattered. She'd learned that lesson the hard way once already; there was no need to relearn it.

"Are you okay?" He was trying to be civil. Could she try? Civil. Nothing further. She nodded.

"And now you know why I thought this job was too dangerous for a woman," he muttered.

Any thoughts of civility faded. He was still a caveman. Worse yet, he was a *pastor* caveman, a profession that would give legitimacy to his "a woman has her place" way of thinking.

Somehow she managed to withhold her response. He meant nothing to her now, so his opinions couldn't hurt her. Theoretically.

Relief flooded Shiloh as she saw a patrol car approaching in the distance. She watched as it crossed the bridge, cringing as she realized it was the chief. She'd hoped they'd send one of the other regular beat cops. The guys would tease her forever for it, but they wouldn't ask probing questions that could reveal her involvement in the case that had killed her cousin.

Annie hadn't been careful enough—and it had gotten her killed. Until Shiloh could figure out why this current string of attacks had begun, she'd need to be on her guard. Someone was keeping tabs on her, and anything she revealed stood the risk of getting back to the wrong person. Not that she didn't trust the chief—she did. But the chance that he might let something slip was too real to ignore. The fewer people who knew about her past, the better. And the safer.

"You okay, Shiloh?" The chief's voice was more gruff than usual, and Shiloh could read his emotions in his tense posture. His gaze moved to Adam.

"I'm fine," she answered. "Though the car has been better. This is—"

"Adam Cole. The new chaplain. Welcome to Treasure Point." The chief surveyed the scene and shook his head. "It's not usually quite so...exciting around here."

Shiloh blinked. Looked to Adam, whose hint of a sheepish grin did nothing to deny the chief's words.

He was the new chaplain? This day couldn't possibly get any worse.

The ride the chief had given Adam and Shiloh into town had been… *Awkward* was too nice a way to put it, Adam thought to himself.

The chief hadn't said much, just had let Shiloh explain what had happened. If Adam wasn't imagining things, she was more nonchalant now than she had been when they'd been in the middle of it. A change in perspective? Or had she been deliberately downplaying the danger?

Adam didn't know, didn't really have time to think about that right now. Shiloh was part of his past—she'd made that very clear when she'd walked away from him years ago with barely a word. He'd moved on—gotten past his broken heart and taken his life in a new direction. His job here was his future, his chance to pastor his own church, have some purpose, maybe even make his dad proud.

He straightened his shoulders before lifting his hand to knock on the solid oak door of Hal Smith's house. He'd talked to the man, and the other deacons, on the phone as part of his interview process but hadn't actually met them in person.

The door opened, revealing a tall bearded man wearing a frown. "You're Reverend Cole?"

"Yes, sir." Adam stuck out his hand. "Nice to meet you."

The other man took it and shook it. Barely. "You're late."

Adam kept his smile affixed and refused to flinch at Hal's obvious displeasure. Yeah, Adam had known this wouldn't make the board happy. Imagine how they would have reacted if the chief hadn't agreed to drive Adam back to his car to retrieve a fresh set of clothes, which he'd changed into at the police station, before he'd arrived. "I'm sorry about that. It won't happen again." Part of him wanted to explain, but his father had taught him not to offer excuses when it came to work, so he didn't.

Another man walked up behind Hal and extended his hand. "Walter Davis. It's nice to meet you, Pastor." He turned to Hal. "Didn't you hear? He was in a wreck on the way here. Give him a break."

Hal made no comment, just grunted and motioned for Adam to come in.

Okay, then. He regrouped and followed the men into the house. The rest of the deacons had gathered in the living room. When Adam entered, they all stood and introduced themselves. Adam noticed that each man wore slacks and a collared shirt, even for an informal meeting like this. Adam did have on a nice golf shirt, but his good jeans seemed out of place. This church might be a little more old-fashioned than he'd realized.

"So, Pastor, how was your trip down?" someone asked.

Adam couldn't help but laugh. "Eventful. I got caught up in traffic and had a couple other problems, but I'm glad to be here."

"Good." They nodded. There was a second's worth of silence, and then Hal, who appeared to be the leader, spoke up again, asking for Adam to share his testimony again with the group, plus what he hoped to accomplish as the pastor of their church. It was information he'd already provided, but Adam didn't mind doing so again in person. Everyone listened attentively, but when Adam was done talking, no one had questions about what he'd said. Instead, they moved the meeting in a different direction entirely.

"We wanted to meet with you immediately to let you know our expectations, now that you're here, so we can have this out face-to-face. You should be aware how important it is that you conduct yourself in an appropriate manner."

Adam's eyebrows rose, and he felt his shoulders tense. "I don't understand what gives you the impression that I wouldn't."

"Our last pastor…" Walter spoke up, shaking his head. "He was asked to leave because of some moral issues."

Adam's heart broke for the church. Losing a pastor for any reason was tough, but to have someone they respected fall prey to sin and leave in such a way… It would be hard for them. He felt himself relax as he realized that, at least in their minds, this was a necessary conversation to have, not an attempt on their part to make him feel uncomfortable the second he got to town. Although it was doing that, as well.

"I understand." Adam nodded. "I can assure all of you that I am a man of integrity, as I told you during my interview process, and as I'm sure my references told you, too."

"Be as that may, Pastor, we have very high standards after what happened."

Their tones, which bordered on accusatory, might have intimidated him when he was straight out of seminary. But he'd had a little time to gain experience as an associate pastor in Atlanta, where he'd started working during his seminary training. He'd seen enough now to realize that they were hurting, that it would take extra care on his part to earn their trust.

But he would earn it. This was his first solo pastoring job. He loved these church members already, even the ones he hadn't met, and he didn't want to let them down. If he failed here, he'd be shortchanging not just his congregants, but his teachers and mentors who believed in him. He hated the thought of that, especially the idea of disappointing his father.

"I'm sure I'll be able to conduct myself in a way that

meets whatever standards you have," he said with confidence, smiling in an attempt to assure them that they didn't need to worry.

Only a couple of them smiled back. Several of them wore straight faces devoid of expression, and one or two were almost frowning.

"I hope you're right," Hal Smith said, finally nodding as he wrapped up the meeting. "I certainly hope you're right."

The words left Adam with an ominous feeling that nearly matched what he'd felt when Shiloh had driven off the road. Of course, he knew he wouldn't back down from the challenges of the position he'd worked so hard to achieve…but the deacons' words left him uneasy. He couldn't help but remember Shiloh's accusation that the earlier attack had been triggered by his arrival.

Just what trouble had he gotten himself into by coming to town?

THREE

Adam waved to the Joneses and kept the smile pasted on his face long enough to get in the car, ease it into Reverse much more gently than he'd wanted to and drive away.

That could have gone better.

Three days on the job and he'd visited four congregation members' houses so far, as the board had requested. The theory was that, as their new pastor, people would want to meet him and get to know him. The visits were also meant to allow him to get to know them.

It was that second part they seemed to be having problems with. Somehow he'd expected this to be easier, even though his dad had warned him that this wouldn't be the case.

"Running a church is harder than you think, son," his dad had told him with a smirk as Adam had prepared to leave Savannah and go to Treasure Point. "You're going to have to give it everything you've got and more."

He was trying. Adam rolled down the windows as he got closer to the marsh. The salty smell reminded him of so many things. Last week's debacle at Hamilton Creek, of course. Adam felt his face tense into a frown. He could still relive the incident in his mind, practically taste the fear he'd felt for their lives, especially Shiloh's. He hadn't spoken to her since then. Nor had he spoken to anyone else about the accident, other than to give his statement to the police.

He wondered if they'd figured out who was behind the accident or if it was even intentional. It had seemed planned to him. But he wasn't a cop. Maybe it was paranoia to worry that someone could be after Shiloh. He had no reason to believe she was in danger. She'd lived a quiet life when he'd known her. Even her current position as a police officer shouldn't be sufficient reason for someone to hurt her. Surely there wasn't a lot of crime in Treasure Point that could result in her making dangerous enemies.

Adam sighed. He didn't know what to think about any of that, so he pushed away the thoughts for now, inhaling another breath of the tangy air. Memories further back in his mind made him think of Savannah's coast. And the time he'd spent there with Shiloh.

Great. Something else he'd failed at.

He prayed that God would do something to help him make an impact in this town. It wasn't as though he'd expected people to start pouring out their life stories to him or divulging their darkest secrets on the first visit. But he hadn't expected them to be so…cordial.

His first Sunday at the church had gone fairly well. The sermon had been well delivered—at least he had thought so. But the people, as they did today, had seemed just short of standoffish. While it was God's word that had the power to change lives, Adam was a firm believer that discipleship was done through deep relationships. Without that, how would he grow this church, succeed in ministry? He'd hoped to feel more secure in his position by today—when the next part of his responsibilities would commence.

He glanced at the clock on the dash. He needed to be at the police station by 12:30 for his first day at that job. Like many small-town churches, this one could only offer enough money for a bi-vocational pastor, so the chaplain position was his second job.

He'd been looking forward to it since he had finished his training several months ago, but now his excitement was being slowly replaced by nerves. If he was having a hard time showing his regular congregation members that he was trustworthy, how would he convince guarded law-enforcement officers that he was someone they could confide in, turn to for counseling?

The drive to the police station went by too fast—he'd been hoping to use the commute to help sort through his thoughts and figure out his next step. Hopefully, the chief had a plan to help Adam persuade people to accept him because Adam was determined to prove he could do this job. To himself and to his father.

The chief's door was open, but Adam knocked anyway.

The man looked up from what he was doing and waved him in. "Ready for your first day?"

"I hope so." He tried to project as much assurance into those words as he could, but judging by the thoughtful expression on the chief's face, Adam had failed.

"Shut that door, would you? Then sit down. I think we should talk."

Adam complied, then had a seat.

"I enjoyed your sermon yesterday."

"Thanks." The words did boost Adam's spirits, but not much. It wasn't the sermons he struggled with; it was the relationship aspect of his job.

"I've been noticing it seems like you're having a little trouble getting to know some folks, though."

The man had to be incredibly observant to have seen that, but then again, with his job, he'd have to be. It shouldn't surprise Adam that the chief's people-watching skills carried over into other areas of life besides the job.

Too bad the chief's notice of such things may likely cost Adam his job before he'd really started. If the chief had doubts about Adam's ability to connect with the police officers, he'd let Adam go before he'd ever been given a chance. Adam couldn't blame him, but he wanted this job. Needed it.

"You're right. It's proving to be a bit of a challenge in some ways, but if you're worried about my ability to be a good chaplain to this department, sir, let me assure you that I am going to give it everything I've got and—"

The chief held up a hand to stop Adam. "That's enough, son. You don't have to defend yourself to me. It's nothing that's your fault anyway. It's how people around here are with outsiders."

It was hard to believe that he could be considered an "outsider" when he'd grown up just over an hour away, but that was how small towns were, he guessed. He was new to Treasure Point, and that was what mattered to these people.

"So what do I do about it?" Adam asked, hating that he needed help but knowing that the chief, of all people, would be able to give him insight into how to succeed at least at this job, if not his pastor job.

The chief rubbed his chin. "I've been working on that question myself. The best thing I can think of to help you here and with the rest of the people from the town is to have you ride along with one of our more respected officers. You'll stay in the car if they're making any calls that seem to warrant extra caution or are obviously dangerous. But you'd ride along on patrol with them anyway."

Adam frowned. "What would that do?" He was willing to do whatever it took, of course, but how could spending time with one man help him make any inroads with anyone else in town?

"When the officers see one of their own trusts you,

they're likely to do so, too. And as the townspeople see you have the stamp of approval from someone they respect, they'll see that they can trust you, too. Make sense?"

The chief's logical explanation had him nodding his head in agreement. "It does, actually."

"So you're fine with that plan?"

"Yes."

The chief stood, clearly happy that they'd worked something out. "Good. There are a few officers I can think of that would work. Officer Evans would have been my first choice, but given the fact that she's in the middle of an investigation into the attack the two of you faced by the bridge, I've decided on Officer Rowland. I'll arrange for you to begin joining him tomorrow." He nodded decisively, the conversation over.

"Wait," Adam heard himself say, even as a plan formed in his mind—one he wasn't sure was smart in any way, but that wouldn't leave his head.

The chief turned to him.

"What if I want to ride with Shiloh—Officer Evans?"

The chief's eyes narrowed a little. "As I said," he replied slowly, "she would have been my first choice. But considering the fact that she could be in danger—and you're an untrained civilian—I don't think that's a good idea."

"I noticed on Saturday that Shiloh rode alone. Was her partner out, or is she always solo?"

"She doesn't have a partner at the moment."

"So there's no one to watch her back." Adam's heart pounded harder as the plan solidified in his mind. "If I'm with her, at least someone will have her six. I'll stay in the car when you think I should, but if you think the attack by the bridge is serious enough to warrant an investigation, then that means she's at risk. And in that case, I want to be there, at least as another set of eyes."

The older man studied him for a full minute or more before speaking. "All right. You can ride with her. But your job as far as protecting her goes no further than being there to call for backup if she's unable to do so. I won't have civilians getting injured in my department. Are we clear?"

Relief and utter fear overwhelmed him. "Yes. Thank you, sir," Adam said as he stood and left the office, his mind still spinning out of control until it finally landed on one clear thought.

Shiloh was going to kill him.

Shiloh returned home after a downright boring shift and sorted through a stack of mail on the counter. Electric bill. Water bill. A letter from an old friend from college.

A hand-addressed envelope. No postage. The sender was in town and wanted to make sure she knew it.

Shiloh dropped the envelope and found her gaze immediately drawn to the window several feet from her. The woods—though they were far in the distance—would make good cover for someone wanting to hide. She felt her skin crawl at the knowledge that she could be standing in the crosshairs of someone's sniper rifle.

She pulled the cord and dropped the blinds, startling at the crash they made as the bottom landed on the windowsill. Every sense went on alert as Shiloh chided herself for being so careless. Someone *had* tried to kill her just days ago and she'd gone about life as though it was business as usual. This wasn't the time to relax. Relaxing got you killed.

She turned, studied the envelope where it sat on the counter. Shiloh weighed her options. Even in a department as small as Treasure Point's, the police station would have tools she didn't have to confirm or deny whether anything dangerous could be sealed inside. But the contents of the letter might include information about her past that she wasn't ready to share. Did she take the risk?

She eyed the envelope again. It was stupid to handle this herself. She knew it was. She knew it when she walked to the cabinet under the kitchen sink where she kept her latex gloves, and when she pulled the collar of her shirt over her mouth and nose as she gently unsealed the letter.

Once it was open, she let out a breath. No suspicious substances, nothing out of the ordinary except for the note inside.

Forget about the past and the people from your past. It won't do anyone any good for you to keep remembering. You don't want to end up like your cousin.

Shiloh choked out a muffled sob at the mention of her cousin. Annie had been just shy of her thirtieth birthday. Too young—much, much too young—to die in the line of duty. But her cousin had eaten, slept and breathed law enforcement and given each case everything she had had. In this instance, that had been her life.

The room spun, and Shiloh closed her eyes to escape it, shoving the note back inside the envelope as she did so. The tone didn't seem blatantly threatening. The first part seemed almost concerned about her; the last line was the only one to speak of danger.

Something didn't feel right. Shiloh shook her head and opened her eyes. Why would this person try to kill her and then send her a warning note? In situations like this, the crimes and attacks usually escalated; they didn't go backward in terms of threat level, as this did. She searched her mind for explanations, something that would make everything clear, but found nothing. Were they toying with her? Trying to confuse and scare her?

Shiloh didn't know.

She left the mail on the counter and walked to her bedroom. She'd take a hot shower, read the book she was in the middle of and see if she could make sense of everything happening in her life. The resurgence of the threat she'd thought had dissipated, Adam's reappearance in her life... It was all too much to take in within a few days.

Yet again she wondered if the two were connected but dismissed the idea. Whoever was threatening her had no connection to Adam—she was certain of that. Adam may be a lot of things—she could make a long, insulting list—but he'd never threaten or attack her. That made one person— two, if she counted the chief—in this town that she could trust if she needed help.

As much as Shiloh preferred to rely on herself, she knew it was smart to have contingency plans. Too bad the one man she felt she could trust the most was the one she'd handed her heart to, only to have it stomped to bits and then returned.

Shiloh turned the shower on to a scalding temperature and breathed in the steam. She always felt better after a good, long shower. Even though these were bigger problems than she'd faced in a while, it would help with those, too, at least a little.

Shiloh was in the middle of shampooing her hair when she heard the first rumble of thunder in the distance. Her long, relaxing shower would have to be a quick one. She hurried her pace and tried to calm the pounding of her heart as the thunder grew louder and more frequent. By the time she had showered and then dressed, rain pelted her little house, and thunder shook the windows violently.

It was a fitting end for the afternoon she'd had, and Shiloh was confident of one thing: it was going to be a very long night.

* * *

Adam sat in his rented house, listening to the howling storm trying to find its way inside. It had succeeded in the kitchen via a leak in the corner of the ceiling. He'd have to fix that once it dried.

He made his way to the garage, eager to work out the tension of the day on his boxing bag. He'd hung it up Sunday afternoon after going back to Savannah following church to pick up his dog, his belongings, which he'd put in a storage unit after moving from Atlanta, and a U-Haul trailer. He hadn't boxed seriously since he'd finished college, but it was the best way he knew to burn off stress. It also helped him focus while he prayed, especially if he was wrestling with something.

Tonight it was Shiloh.

He'd seen her in town once or twice, but they hadn't spoken since that first day. Not that it seemed to matter to Adam's heart or mind. He kept thinking of her, of the way things used to be. Wondering if she was in danger now. Wishing he could do something to protect her if she was. His tumultuous thoughts about her made it difficult for him to focus on anything else.

He'd been in love with her once—before she'd broken his heart by leaving him behind. It had been a shock to see her again, putting his emotions in turmoil. But he wasn't one to let feelings overrule his common sense. They were at different places in life now. He'd seen a hardness in her eyes that hadn't been there before, and he knew he'd changed, too. It wasn't as if picking up where they'd left off was a good idea or an option at all.

Besides, she'd run away from him once. He wasn't exactly eager to experience that again, especially when he wasn't clear on all the details of why she'd left. Everything had been perfect in their relationship; but in the last six months of Shiloh's cousin's life, things had started to change between him and Shiloh. The three of them had all been friends, but eventually Shiloh and Annie had started getting together alone and making it clear that he wasn't welcome. Shiloh had given only vague answers when he'd asked about their evenings. Now he wondered if he should have pressed her more.

And then there had been that blowup in his dad's office, days after Annie's death, when Shiloh had gone to his dad for help, and he'd told her that what she was planning— becoming a cop to find her cousin's killers herself and pursue justice—was wrong, even unbiblical for a woman.

That seemed to be the moment things ended for them.

He punched the bag hard.

He pulled back to do it again when his cell phone rang. He slowed his breathing and answered. It was a man from his church whose teenage daughter was about to have emergency surgery for appendicitis. From what Adam gathered, it sounded as though the situation was under control, but people liked to have a pastor around in those cases.

He ran upstairs and jumped in the shower, ignoring the crashing thunder and deciding getting struck by lightning while wet in his bathroom would be better than going out in public smelling as though he'd been working out for an hour.

Adam felt relieved that the man had called and had given Adam an excuse to stop thinking about Shiloh in particular and women in law enforcement in general. For tonight he was grateful to put them both out of his mind.

FOUR

Shiloh was beyond ready to get to work the next morning. The storm the night before had set her on edge. Along with the threatening note, the weather had unearthed memories she'd thought long buried. The crashing thunder had sounded the same as it had on the night Annie had been killed. Shiloh had lain awake all night, caught between the past and the present. Even if she'd been inclined to heed the warnings of the note found in her mailbox, she couldn't forget the past. It was etched in her memory with the clarity of a lightning flash.

This morning, as she navigated her new cruiser toward the station, she considered her options. Running was not one of them, as far as she was concerned. If they'd bothered to track her here, they'd track her anywhere, and she didn't want to live life continually looking over her shoulder. Besides, as part of the law-enforcement community, she could keep an eye on things. Wasn't that the reason she'd left behind her job as a history professor and had become a cop?

Her cousin's face flashed in her mind. Keeping an eye on things wasn't the only reason. Shiloh owed it to Annie to finish what she had started.

Maybe Shiloh was looking at this wrong.

Regardless, she didn't have time to worry about it right

now. She parked her car and entered the police station in time for roll call, when the day's assignments were given out. She learned she'd be patrolling an area near Widow Hamilton's house that included several miles of Treasure Point's coastal marshes.

"Officer Evans, the chief needs to see you in his office. Anyone have questions?"

Lieutenant Rich Davies scanned the room, brows raising when he came to Shiloh as though he expected her to have a question. Her cheeks burned with a blush she hoped no one noticed; she felt like a kid who'd been called out for talking in class. She hadn't been paying attention but wasn't going to give him the satisfaction of admitting it.

The meeting was dismissed, and Shiloh walked to the chief's door and knocked. Uneasy flutters danced in her stomach as she tried to figure out what he could want.

"Come in."

She pushed the door open, willing away the tumultuous thoughts while forcing a pleasant smile on her face. "You wanted to see me?"

The chief nodded. Shiloh stepped in to take a seat when she noticed that one of the desk chairs was occupied. Her step faltered. "I can come back later if you're already in a meeting." That sandy-blond hair could belong to only one person.

"No, now's a fine time." The chief cleared his throat. "Lieutenant Davies already give out assignments for the day?"

Shiloh nodded as she sat.

"What I told him I'd tell you myself is that you have something of an extra assignment for the next several weeks."

The flutters in her stomach returned full force.

"You already know Adam is the new chaplain…"

With the words "extra assignment" and "Adam" in such close proximity, the flutters turned to concrete bricks. There was no good way for this to turn out. Shiloh straightened in her chair, listening closely. There had to be a way to get out of whatever her commanding officer was suggesting; she never gave up without a fight.

The chief shifted in his chair. "What you may not realize is the difficulty of a man in his position. He's here to help the department and the town, and he can't do that if he doesn't know people, doesn't fit in like a local. For the next few weeks I'm assigning Adam to ride along with you. As you get the chance, tell him about the town, introduce him to people. As the other officers see you accepting him, they'll start to. Everyone loves you, Shiloh. They look to you." The chief nodded as though he was as pleased with his decision as Shiloh was displeased. "Do this for me and for Adam, would you?"

"Sir, I'm flattered that you think this would help him, but wouldn't my time be better spent pursuing whoever tried to run me off the road the other day? Or checking out Widow Hamilton's house for her?"

"Your time is best spent doing what I've asked you to do." The chief's voice was still kind, but she could hear the steel in it. Nothing about this was optional.

Or fair, in Shiloh's opinion.

"I understand the two of you knew each other in Savannah. I would think you'd be eager to help out an old friend."

Shiloh's eyes darted to Adam as the chief spoke. Was it her imagination or was there a degree of pleading in those gorgeous eyes? Once upon a time those eyes had melted her like chocolate on a hot summer day. Even now their effect was difficult to resist.

She let out a breath. "You're right. It's the least I can do to help an old friend."

The chief nodded, the matter settled to him. "Good."

Shiloh could feel Adam's eyes on her and knew if she looked she would read his thanks in them. But the fact that she couldn't bring herself to intentionally hurt him like he'd hurt her didn't mean she was ready to buddy up to him, either. Without another word to either man, she started for the door.

"And, Officer Evans?"

Shiloh turned.

The chief leaned back in his chair, folded his arms behind his head and grinned. "Try to keep this car intact."

She made a face. "I'll do my best."

Adam followed her to the parking lot. At least, Shiloh assumed he did so. She certainly didn't wait for him, but when she unlocked the car doors, they both climbed in. She turned the key in the ignition and drove toward the area she had been assigned to patrol.

At least her shift today was seven to three. She'd be home well before dinner, safely inside before darkness sneaked in. Logically speaking, she was no safer during the day, as the attacks on her so far had already proved. But darkness reminded her of the night Annie had been killed.

"Beautiful scenery."

What was he, Chatty Cathy? Why did the man feel compelled to talk?

She grunted in response. Men could do it, so maybe it would work for her.

"Shiloh…" He shifted in the seat beside her, and his tone said more than a dozen words could have. He touched her arm. Her breath caught and she stiffened. "Look, it was years ago. Whatever happened, can't you let it go? Or do you hate me that much?"

Adam hadn't realized how much touching her—even on the arm—would affect him. His heart drummed a crazy rhythm in his chest, and he knew reaching out to her had been a bad idea.

But how was she reacting? Did he still affect her at all? She'd gone rigid when he had first rested his hand on her arm, but she was softening now, relaxing. No, whatever she was telling herself, he knew the truth. She didn't hate him at all.

Relief battled with tension in his shoulders. Her not hating him made this much more dangerous. All he wanted was to make sure that she stayed safe. Maybe be friends with her again.

He'd already experienced firsthand the heartbreak she was capable of inflicting. He wasn't eager to sign up for round two.

"Can't we forget the past?" he asked.

Her pause was so long that he was sure she'd say no or have some kind of comeback for him. But, instead, after a minute of ear-deafening, heart-pounding silence, her answer stunned him.

"Okay." She let out a breath. "I'll try."

Adam wanted to say so much more but only nodded and said, "I'm glad."

He glanced over at her, as he thought about how much had changed since the past he'd just promised to forget. She wasn't the Shiloh he'd known. That Shiloh had been a bit of a risk-taker, sure. She'd loved to go rock climbing and whitewater rafting, and she had even talked him into hang gliding up in north Georgia once. But she'd been sweet, gentle and not at all the intimidating, in-charge woman she appeared to be now. It seemed she'd left that personality in the past along with her history-professor job.

Something niggled in his stomach. Gut instinct told him the changes in her personality, her job, were somehow tied to whatever reasons she'd had for breaking up with him five years ago. Adam had never considered himself dumb when it came to women, but those few months of Shiloh's life, the last few months of their relationship, had been so hectic with Annie's death and Shiloh's reaction to it that he'd never known what had made them hit their breaking point. All she had said was that they weren't right for each other. At the time he'd been too stunned to press for more of an explanation, but now that she was back in his life, he intended to get an answer eventually to replace the question mark that hovered in his mind, if only to satisfy his curiosity.

Riding along with her would help him achieve two goals. He'd finally get some answers—and he'd be close at hand to help if any more attacks materialized. He may have put the past behind him and moved on from his feelings for Shiloh, but he was still determined to make sure she stayed safe.

Shiloh pulled the car off into a secluded parking area next to another stretch of Hamilton Creek. In town, where he'd seen the creek before, it looked like any other creek. A little marshy but pretty civilized in general.

Here the water flowed freely through the reeds and grass. It was guarded by centuries-old oak trees—whose creaky branches were draped with gray Spanish moss—and Georgia pines taller than he could guess. Adam could smell the salt in the air coming through his rolled-down window and figured they must be close to the coast.

"Is the ocean near here?" he asked Shiloh.

She nodded. "A hundred yards or so through some of the thickest coastal forest you've ever seen."

"Ever walked to the beach from here?"

Shiloh raised her eyebrows. "It's not a beach like you're thinking. Not sandy like Tybee. There's a little sand, but mostly the water meets the marsh, and that's the end of that. And, no, I've never walked from here. There are some trails not too far from here, half a mile or so away, but it's too dangerous to try from here. The woods are chock-full of snakes, and it's so thick it would be easy to get lost."

"That doesn't sound like my adventurer."

She speared him with a look before turning away and opening her car door. "I'm not *your* anything anymore, Adam, except maybe your friend, and that's still kind of probationary."

Probationary? She'd always liked big words, but they'd been words like *historicity.* She even talked like a cop now.

"I see." He opened his door to follow her. "So, where are we going?"

"I'm not sure you should be going anywhere." She frowned, looked at the car and then back at him as if deliberating what she should do.

"Worried I'll slow you down?" He couldn't resist the urge to tease her. She'd always been competitive, and it had grated on her anytime he had managed to finish a hike before her, which was often. Shiloh was in great shape, but his boxing days had made him even more fit, and since exercise was a stress reliever for him, he hadn't lost much muscle tone since.

"No, but aren't you supposed to be riding along and getting out if I'm talking to a townsperson? This is more like investigating."

"I'll be fine. Tell me about where we are."

Shiloh seemed to consider it, then shrugged. "It's your call. This is one of the areas closest to Widow Hamilton's home. She's kind of town royalty, I guess, or as close as we get in south Georgia. Her family was among the founders of the town, and their homestead is almost as old as the dirt it's built on. Anyway, she's had trouble lately—prowlers, or so she thinks."

"What do you mean, 'so she thinks'?"

Shiloh frowned again.

What was it about him that made the woman frown so much? He was going to have to work on ways to get her to flash that brilliant smile she had.

"Honestly, I think she's probably a lonely old woman with a big imagination. But I feel bad that I can't do more to make her feel better, so I'm hoping that telling her I checked out this area—since it's adjacent to her property—and came up empty will put her mind at ease."

Adam nodded. "Got it. Sounds fun. Let's go."

"It could be dangerous. As a civilian, I feel like you should know that. I would hate to put you in danger."

She sounded passionate about that last line, as if she spoke from experience. Another aspect of this new Shiloh that mystified him.

"I'm sure we'll be fine." He spoke with confidence, but as she finally started off toward the edge of the woods, and he followed her, he felt eyes on him again.

And had the distinct impression that, despite her best efforts, they were in danger already.

"Hey, Shiloh?" He lowered his voice and continued to follow her, not breaking the rhythm of his stride. "Do you feel at all like we're being watched?"

Shiloh didn't look back. But Adam saw her nod. Chills crawled up his spine, and he found himself hoping they were only being viewed through something innocuous like binoculars. And not through the scope of a high-powered rifle.

Shiloh reached the edge of the woods and began to inspect the perimeter, seeking footprints or other signs of recent activity. She walked slowly along the tree line, scanning around her as she went. Adam kept an eye out, too, but when it came down to it, although he wanted to be protecting her, she was the one with the training and the gun. If any real danger arose, *she* would be the one keeping *him* safe. He'd always liked the idea of men being the protectors—an old-fashioned idea Shiloh and Annie had always teased him about. It wasn't that he thought women were incapable—not at all—he just liked the idea of men filling that role.

He remembered Shiloh and his father debating the same thing after her cousin's death. He wouldn't say that his opinions were as extreme as his father's, but Adam hadn't contradicted his dad or said anything to support Shiloh's position. He was sure he hadn't imagined the flash of fire in Shiloh's eyes as she'd said good-night after that long-ago discussion.

He'd told Shiloh to forget the past, so why was he having such a hard time keeping it from crowding in on him? Adam pushed the memories from his mind in time to avoid running into Shiloh, who had stopped cold in front of the oddest pine tree he'd ever seen. Its trunk grew straight for the first ten feet or so, made a dramatic almost-ninety-degree turn to the left for a stretch and then continued growing upward.

"Weird tree, huh?"

"Shhh." She pressed a finger to her lips and motioned to the ground.

At first glance he didn't understand what had caught her eye. He saw only grass, pine needles and palmettos. A second look told him that everything was pressed to the ground as if this had been used as a pathway.

A third look revealed something at the base of a palmetto plant. He leaned closer.

The color was duller than it would have been in a movie, likely because of its probable age, but there in the dirt he saw the unmistakable gleam of a gold Spanish doubloon.

FIVE

"Is that…?"

"Shhh!" Shiloh glared at her companion. Adam's voice wasn't raised, but it sounded obnoxiously loud to her ears. She knew she was being jumpy, but the unease she'd felt since they had left the car—that hard-to-pinpoint-why feeling that someone was watching them—had grown since she had spotted the gold coin on the ground.

She'd blinked several times when it had first caught her eye, not willing to believe that it was real. Yet judging by Adam's reaction, she wasn't the only one seeing it.

Shiloh had studied another gold coin like this just one other time in her life. Her cousin had shown it to Shiloh on the night that Annie had been killed. Annie had said it was evidence in the case they were building against the men who had turned into killers in their quest for an old pirate treasure—the case Shiloh had been consulting on against her better judgment. Apparently, the criminals had found a few gold coins somewhere near Savannah, and that was what had inspired them to look for the rumored large treasure Blackbeard had hidden around the same area. They'd branched out into murder not long afterward with the suspicious death of a port-authority officer.

There had been other victims—men who had, evidently, gotten in the killers' way. Annie had put the pieces together.

"Shiloh," Annie had said, eyes gleaming, "all we have to do now is find where the treasure is, and the men will come to us."

Instead, Annie had been the last known victim.

A hand on Shiloh's arm brought her every sense to high alert, and it was all she could do to hold back her scream. Adam jerked away his hand, his wide eyes looking at her as if she were losing her mind. Maybe she was. But that coin on the ground was the past and the present all colliding in a hundred different ways, and Shiloh wasn't ready for it. Couldn't do it again.

"Do we pick it up or leave it?"

"Pick it up." Shiloh pulled out her smartphone, snapped a picture to note the exact positioning, then reached in her pocket, retrieved a tissue and gingerly pinched the coin between two fingers before dropping it into a small paper bag she kept in her pocket in case situations like this one arose. "It may be evidence."

"Evidence that people are prowling around that widow's house?"

Shiloh's thoughts hadn't been on her shift or Widow since the moment she had seen that doubloon, but she nodded. It was evidence of that, too. She glanced to her right, to the trails that she knew led eventually to the edge of the Hamilton property. Maybe the older woman wasn't imagining things after all. "I'll let the chief know we need to keep an eye on her and take her calls seriously."

She spun on her heel and walked back to the car as fast as she could. The coin could be a trap, could have been placed there by someone who knew that she wouldn't be able to resist the urge to pick it up and see if it matched the one found by her cousin. Her history knowledge told her it did, though. It bore all the markings of a coin of the same era, and the irregularities in the edges looked to be genuine.

After what seemed like forever, they reached the area where she'd parked the car. Without looking up, Shiloh dug into her pocket for the keys, clicked the unlock button and reached for the door.

"Stop."

Adam's firm grip on her arm was nothing like the gentle touch from earlier.

She spun her head to look at him. "What?" She heard the snap in her tone but couldn't stop it.

He said nothing, just pointed to the car. She followed with her eyes.

Several of the windows were smashed in. The tires had been viciously sliced. And spray-painted across the front window were the words "Forget the past," and on the rear window were the words "or end up like your cousin."

The dizziness that overtook her had nothing to do with the heat or the fact that she'd skipped breakfast. As Shiloh fought to regain control over her body, Adam didn't let go of her arm. He stood still and steadied her. He was there for her, solid in the middle of circumstances that made her feel as if she'd waded deep into south Georgia quicksand and was being sucked in whole.

"I'd better call the chief." She pulled herself away from Adam, already missing his strength.

"Chief? This is Officer Evans," she said into her cell phone, not wanting to bother with dispatch when this was a situation the chief needed to know about directly. She hardly recognized the voice as hers. Inside she was shaking and scared out of her mind, but outside she was capable. Confident.

She didn't want the men who were after her to see how she really felt.

"Is there trouble?"

"Yes. I'm over near Hamilton Point, on the edge of my

patrol area. I wanted to make sure there was no sign of prowlers using the coastal trails to get to the widow's house."

"And you found a sign?"

She swallowed hard. "Yes. I did. But I'm calling to tell you I need backup. My car's been vandalized, and the warning on it says we better take this seriously."

"I'll have men there in five minutes."

"Thank you, sir." Shiloh slid the phone back into its holster, letting her right hand rest on the grip of her gun.

"You really think you're going to need it?"

Adam's calm question grated on her. "If I didn't, would I carry it at all? It's better to be prepared."

He shrugged. "Couldn't what happened to the car be a simple case of vandalism?"

"With the mention of Annie?"

"But the rest doesn't make any sense. 'Forget the past'?"

Shiloh's heartbeat quickened as she thought back to the case that had cost Annie her life. She'd been so hesitant to get involved herself and wouldn't have if her cousin hadn't desperately needed someone she could trust to help find answers, to keep the case confidential. Because of that Shiloh had decided that the fewer people who knew about it, the better. Had she really never told Adam, who had been her fiancé, what she'd been up to?

"It's a lot to explain."

"I have time."

She shook her head. "Not now. I have to focus on everything around us, keep my head in the game. I can't do that if we talk about Savannah."

She scanned the landscape, wondering why she bothered. This was a sniper's paradise with the tall grass and the shadowy forest looming thirty yards away from where she'd parked. If someone had wanted her dead right now, they'd have shot her already. Besides, the spray-painted words appeared to be a warning, designed to scare her out of investigating the case any further.

Though Shiloh could feel fear threatening to overtake her, the vandal's words didn't accomplish their intended purpose. Instead, they steeled her resolve to finally find out who was behind these attacks and her cousin's murder.

Shiloh noted that Adam didn't try to convince her to discuss the past. His slow nod told her that he respected her decision to change the subject. Shiloh's heart warmed at how he didn't push.

They stood in silence, Shiloh fighting against the fear that still threatened under the surface of her forced calm. She felt herself relax as she watched a patrol car pull in next to hers several minutes later.

"Man, Shiloh, who'd you make mad?" Officer Matt O'Dell whistled to punctuate his words. "You must've ticked somebody off good."

Shiloh laughed, feeling the tension ease the way it always did when O'Dell was involved. He was a Southern good old boy to the core, with the thicker-than-molasses accent to prove it. "Apparently." Her gaze fell on the car, and she read the message again. There was no pretending that the attacks on her weren't related to her past, not anymore. The murderers who had tracked her here, to the sleepy seaside town of Treasure Point, were still tracking her every move.

And they wanted to make sure she knew that.

Adam had said he felt as if they were being watched. Was she being watched all the time? Was someone watching even now? Would she drive home from work tonight, let herself into her house, thinking she was safe, not realizing she was mere feet away from someone watching her from outside, maybe through a window?

The idea made her skin crawl.

"I don't see anyone." Officer Clay Hitchcock lowered the binoculars he'd been using to canvass the area. "Whoever did this is either well hidden or already gone."

"In cases like this, where someone makes things personal, doesn't the person harassing them usually stick around to see the reaction?" Shiloh asked.

Hitchcock shrugged. "Maybe. But it is a little odd. It makes it odder that this isn't the first thing that's happened to you lately. Any idea what the message means?"

"Yeah," O'Dell interrupted. "We heard about your little swim in the creek. You think the two things are coincidence? Or related?" He cocked his head to the side and waited. Shiloh decided to avoid answering Hitchcock's question and answer O'Dell's. Maybe no one would notice.

"Related. Things like this don't happen often enough for the two to be unconnected." There. That was a good explanation. There was no need to tell them that she had a good idea why she was being targeted. Whoever had done this was undoubtedly the person or persons who had killed her cousin.

The question was...why now? And did it have anything to do with the fact that Adam had walked back into her life for the first time in five years? She couldn't see a logical connection, but the coincidence was overwhelming. She'd lived for years in Treasure Point, not going to any dramatic lengths to disguise her identity or cover her trail. A motivated criminal should have had her cornered within months of her leaving Savannah. Instead, they'd waited. But why? Why now? And since Annie had found evidence of their crimes only in Savannah, why here?

The only connection she could think of was a conversation in the break room at the police department during lunch not long ago. The talk had turned to pirates, and Shiloh had mentioned several facts about Blackbeard and his supposed stash of hidden gold. From there the conversation had turned to the police officers who had been killed five years ago in Savannah as part of a treasure hunt. She hadn't admitted her involvement in it. But had something she'd said given her away?

She shuddered at the idea that one of her fellow officers could be involved with the criminals who had killed her cousin. No, there had to be another explanation.

Shiloh stared at the car as the other officers inspected it and the surrounding area for evidence. It was probably too much to hope that the vandal had dropped the can of spray paint or done something equally stupid, but it was always good to check.

Shiloh surveyed the damage again, noting then the seats inside the car had been shredded and stuffing pulled from them. Had they been looking for something? That made the least amount of sense of any of her theories. If they thought she had something they needed, they wouldn't have waited five years to get it. Especially from a cruiser she had just acquired a few hours ago.

The chief would have to know her suspicions eventually. But to tell the chief risked someone at the station overhearing. What if her suspicions about a connection between the recent attacks and that seemingly harmless pirate-treasure conversation were correct? She needed a safe sounding board, someone not connected to the department. Someone to help her think through everything.

She looked over at Adam, who stood off to the side. Did she dare?

Shiloh glanced back at the car, then down at the wrapped gold doubloon in her hand. Hardly any time had passed since this nightmare had begun again, and already she'd feared for her life several times. It was only going to get worse.

"Why don't you two hop in the back? I've got a call in to Bernie at the tow place, and he should be here soon. In the meantime, I'm sure the chief has lots of questions for you." Clay Hitchcock opened the back door of the cruiser and motioned for them to climb in.

Shiloh only hoped she had enough clever ways to avoid some of those questions.

They rode to the station in silence. Shiloh spent the time thinking through everything she would need to do.

She could remember what had made her first become a history major in college. She'd always been fascinated with the past, with the stories history could tell. One day she'd heard the famous phrase that *those who don't study history are doomed to repeat it,* and she'd realized she wanted to learn from the past and help others do the same.

In this case, if she didn't learn from the past, parts of it were going to be repeated. But, as in the study of the history of cultures, studying her history was going to require walking back through it. Reliving it.

Shiloh shivered. She wasn't sure yet if she had what it took to do that.

"The chief is expecting you," Hitchcock told her as they pulled up in front of the building.

Shiloh nodded and climbed out of the car. Adam followed her. Should she dismiss him, or might the chief want to talk to him, too? She'd wait and let the chief decide.

She felt eyes on her as soon as they walked into the building, felt the infamy that came from essentially wrecking two department cars in the span of four days. This was why she couldn't tell the chief. This department had no secrets.

And Shiloh had more than her share.

"Officer Evans. Have a seat," the chief instructed when

she reached his office. "Reverend Cole, do you mind staying, giving me your side of what happened?"

Shiloh saw Adam's silent agreement, and for some crazy reason she couldn't explain, she felt herself relaxing at the knowledge that he wasn't leaving her.

"Now, why don't you start at the beginning?"

Shiloh filled the chief in on all the details, from the moment they'd pulled the car over, to finding the coin, to discovering that the car had been vandalized.

"I think I'm in agreement with Officer O'Dell that you've made somebody angry."

"So you think this is related to the attack by the bridge?"

He nodded. "It's unusual that you'd be almost killed and then threatened, rather than the other way around. But, yes, I see no reason to believe they're separate incidents."

Just what she'd been afraid of. And she hadn't even told him about the note she'd received at her house.

"Anything you need to tell me, Shiloh?" He switched from his gruff-boss tone to the gentler one that made him a father figure to half the men in the department.

"Not at the moment, sir." Which was true. He didn't need to know yet.

He eyed her for another second and then leaned back, his classic signal that the conversation was over.

"All right. Then get back on your shift. I've switched your area for now. Hitchcock will cover that region, and you'll be in town."

She nodded, relief flooding through her.

"Reverend, I was going to have you ride with her for the whole shift today, but if you're up for it, some of the men here are going out to lunch in a little while at a local barbecue joint, and it might be a good chance for you to get to know them."

Adam nodded. "That sounds great, sir." His eyes flickered to Shiloh. "Unless you think someone should be with Officer Evans today? After what's happened?"

The chief chuckled. "She's got dozens of rounds of forty caliber for that gun on her hip, and she sure knows how to use it. I'm not worried about Shiloh."

Shiloh forced a smile and tried to regain some sense of calm. The chief was right. Adam was a chaplain, not an officer. He didn't need to be assigned to some ridiculous protective detail.

But as she stood up to leave the room, she realized with startling clarity that being with Adam made her feel…safe.

Yes, he'd broken her heart. But he was a man of honor. And she knew without a doubt that the ideas she'd had before driving into town—ideas of sharing the events of the past with Adam and getting his perspective—weren't as crazy as she'd worried they were.

"Thanks, though. And, Adam?" She smiled, her pulse quickening as she thought about the way she was about to give her trust to a man who had so thoroughly let her down before. "If you don't mind dropping by, say around six, to help fix that loose board on my front deck, I'll feed you for your trouble."

Confusion muddled his face for half a second, as she'd suspected it would, and then understanding dawned, and he nodded. "I'll be there."

SIX

Adam was sure the day couldn't have dragged on any longer. The uncertain look Shiloh had worn as she'd invited him over, the vulnerability in her blue eyes, haunted him. He hoped he'd been pleasant enough during lunch with the guys. The chief had even joined them. Adam remembered laughing, talking and answering questions, but all the while Shiloh had been there in the back of his mind.

Several of the officers had heard about the incidents Shiloh and her cars had met with in the past four days and were interested to hear Adam's take on them. After Adam had recounted them to the eager listeners, the chief had shaken his head and had admitted he was worried about Shiloh. The rest of the guys had laughed, citing numerous examples that proved she was more than capable of taking care of herself.

Adam could sympathize with the chief, though. Clearly she enjoyed the job, but he'd always felt this kind of work was unacceptably dangerous. He admired the commitment of the men and women who were willing to serve, but it wasn't a position he wanted to see filled by anyone he cared for. He'd thought her cousin's death would have proved that to Shiloh, too, but, instead, losing Annie was the catalyst that had made Shiloh seek out the same job that had cost her cousin her life.

Women didn't make sense.

Adam pulled his car into the driveway of his little rental house and checked the clock on the dash before shutting off the engine. He was cutting it close. It was five-thirty now, and he'd hoped to clean up a little before heading over to Shiloh's.

He'd been uncomfortable all afternoon, worrying about her safety and wondering why she'd become a target. The note on her car had mentioned her cousin. Annie had been gone for five years, since long before Shiloh started this job. What did Annie have to do with the danger Shiloh was in now?

Adam was ready for some answers.

"Hey, Tux." He opened the door and greeted his boxer, who was wagging his tail so eagerly it was a wonder the thing didn't fall off. "Sorry, buddy. I'm not home for long. I have a date." He could hardly believe the words as he said them aloud, and apparently Tux couldn't, either, because his enthusiasm didn't fade. Of course, the dog may have wanted dinner more than Adam's company, and Tux knew Adam wouldn't leave without feeding the dog first.

He petted Tux on the head, grabbed his supersize bag of dog food from the bottom of the pantry and dumped a generous amount in the dog's bowl. The way Tux tore into the food as if he hadn't eaten in weeks, Adam was surprised Tux hadn't learned yet how to open the pantry door and get it himself.

Leaving the dog to his dinner, Adam hurried to his bedroom, where he changed into a clean pair of jeans and a shirt. Then he told the dog goodbye, locked up and walked to his car.

As he pulled into her driveway minutes later, his heart started to pound. This house was exactly what he'd pictured her living in. Complete with a front porch and rocking chairs. It made him think of the home he'd once hoped they'd share. Was he fooling himself to think he'd gotten over the pain of losing that dream?

Whether this was a dumb idea or not—getting involved in Shiloh's life again—he couldn't sit idly by while she was at risk, no matter how dangerous the close proximity to her felt to his traitorous, untrustworthy heart. He parked the car and sat, taking one deep breath after another.

His phone rang as he was working on getting up the guts to go inside. Adam glanced down at the screen. It was his dad. He pushed back the temptation to ignore it. His dad would keep calling until he got an answer.

"Hello?"

"Adam! How are you, son?"

"I'm good. How are you?"

"Things here are fine. The same as always. I want to hear about you. How's the new church going? How do you like Treasure Point? I liked it the few times I went to visit family there."

Some cousins had been in the area for years until they'd moved to Florida last spring. They'd attended Creekview Church and had been friends with many on the deacon board. Those connections were part of the reason he'd been given this job when he had little pastoral experience so far.

"It's going okay. You know how it is getting to know people, getting them to trust you..." Adam trailed off.

"I don't know how it is, Adam. You're called to be there, so you owe it to those people to make an effort to be the pastor they need. Are you going on a pastoral call tonight? Should I let you go?"

If only Adam could say yes—get off the phone and look good in front of his dad, killing two birds with one stone.

"No, I'm done working for the day." He wished he didn't feel guilty as he said that. He'd worked his shift at the police department that morning and gone straight from there to the church. It was well over an eight-hour day, not exactly slacker's hours, although his dad probably would disagree.

"So you're having dinner at home?" He laughed. "If I remember right, your culinary skills are a little lacking. See? Making pastoral visits would get you out of cooking, too."

Adam didn't know why he said it. Knew he shouldn't but couldn't hold it back any longer. "Actually, I'm not cooking tonight. I'm having dinner with a friend." His heart pounded. Here it came...

"A friend? Who?"

Adam had known his dad would ask. "With Shiloh Evans."

"Shiloh? What is she doing in Treasure Point?"

"She's working here."

"As a cop."

It wasn't a question, the way his dad had said it.

"Adam—" his voice was filled with warning "—men are designed to be protectors. Not women. Didn't you learn anything from what happened with your mom?"

"I'm not talking about Mom with you right now, Dad."

"Fine. Let's not talk about her. Let's talk about Shiloh. She breaks your heart, then becomes a cop when she knows how you and I feel about it."

It crossed Adam's mind that Dad actually hadn't *known* how Adam had felt about it. Everyone had just assumed that he and his dad agreed.

"And now you're thinking of restarting a relationship there? When you're a *pastor* now? Son, a pastor's wife—"

"No one is talking marriage, Dad."

"Fine. A pastor's *girlfriend* is subject to all kinds of unsaid standards you know nothing about. You think Shiloh's going to bake a casserole for a potluck dinner, take banana bread to sick congregation members, help you do ministry when she's too caught up in carrying a gun and seeking revenge?"

Adam's gut churned. "I never said anything about dating her."

"But if you're seeing her again—"

Adam did something he rarely did. He cut his dad off. "Look, Dad. I'm not dating her. You're probably right that she wouldn't make a suitable match for a pastor. But I'm not dating Shiloh. We're friends. Barely even that. I'm doing her a favor, fixing her broken porch."

And trying to keep her safe and figure out why a killer was after her. But Adam had wised up over the past few minutes—he'd keep that part secret. There were some things his dad didn't need to know.

"I'll let you go, then." His dad's tone had softened a little. "Adam, I'm not trying to interfere. I'm just proud of you being a pastor. It's a hard job that I want to be as easy for you as possible. Not like it was for me because of the career your mother—"

"I told you I'm not talking about her." Adam forced the words out, fought back the sadness that he knew would come in waves if he let it.

"Fine. But I warned you."

The line clicked.

Adam dropped the phone into the seat as if it had burned him. And in some ways it had. He wished he could go back in time, not answer that call, not have his dad's advice echoing in his head. But that was the thing about the past. You couldn't change it, so it was better just to move on. Taking a deep breath, he climbed out of the car and walked to Shiloh's front door, raising his hand to knock.

She opened the door and smiled. Oddly enough, he felt some of his stress melt away in the light of her smile.

Shiloh looked gorgeous. Too gorgeous for his own good.

Her dark hair was pulled back into a messy ponytail, and she was wearing a T-shirt, ripped jeans and flip-flops.

"Hi!" She was still grinning as she scanned his clothes. He'd opted for jeans but had put on a polo instead of a T-shirt, because for some reason he didn't want her to think he was a total slob in his after-work hours. "You look nice. Sure you don't mind fixing my porch in that?"

He shook his head.

"The porch will actually only take a second. It was really just an excuse to get you over here. But if you don't mind nailing in this new board while I finish dinner, that would be great."

"I'll be back in when it's done, then." He motioned to the two-by-four in the corner. "That's the new one?"

"Yep. That one over there—" she motioned to the edge of the porch "—is getting seriously warped by the water coming off the roof when it rains."

He nodded, making a mental note to fix the drainage problem so she wouldn't be facing this problem regularly. "Got it. It'll just take a few minutes."

Shiloh started back inside but paused in the doorway. "Hey, Adam?"

He looked up and was rewarded with the sweetest smile he'd seen in five years. "Yeah?"

"Thanks for doing this." She rubbed her right hand over her empty left-hand ring finger. On purpose or subconsciously? "I know you don't owe me anything, and you're probably pretty mad at me. For leaving like I did. But thank you."

And then she was gone. And Adam was finding it hard to be too mad about the past.

That couldn't be good.

Shiloh let the screen door slam behind her, certain she couldn't stand there looking at Adam for another minute without falling in love with him all over again. There were thousands of reasons that this was a terrible idea, though at the moment she couldn't think of one of them.

She brushed a stray strand of hair out of her face, suddenly self-conscious about the way she looked. Had Adam dressed up for her? He looked distractingly good; she'd always loved dark green on him. Was that why he'd picked that shirt?

If she didn't have chicken to fry and potatoes to mash, she'd be tempted to change into something stunning that would make his heart do all the crazy things hers was doing. Just as well that she was starving. The old attraction between them was better off left alone.

She mixed the cream cheese into the potatoes—part of her mom's secret recipe—and struggled to keep Adam from her mind. What had she been thinking, inviting him over? It had seemed like such a good idea earlier and like an even better idea after hearing how uneasy the chief had sounded about the recent incidents.

Assurance returned. She had to sort this out somehow, and she'd always worked better with a partner, someone to bounce ideas off of and to view things differently. She and Annie had been perfect together. This pirate case wasn't the only one that Annie had talked through with her, but it had been Shiloh's first official job as a consultant. It had matched perfectly with her previous career, her specialty in early American history and pirate legends.

Though she'd always loved analyzing things with her cousin over late-night coffee, Shiloh had hesitated to get involved in this case officially, even off the record. She'd told her cousin no at first, but when Annie's overtures were rejected by several other professors at the college where Shiloh had worked, Shiloh had felt she had no other choice.

She'd even gone to Professor Slate—her mentor and the

newly appointed head of the history department—asking him to reconsider and to help her cousin. He'd refused, citing all of the responsibilities he had at the university. Shiloh had understood, of course, but she'd wished anybody else could've helped. As much as she loved adventurous hobbies, she hadn't wanted to get involved in a case that had already involved three murders by the time Annie had asked for Shiloh's help.

Ultimately, and against her better judgment, she had gotten involved. But she hadn't been able to figure anything out fast enough to prevent a fourth murder. If Shiloh didn't get help soon, she wouldn't be able to stop a fifth murder.

Hers.

The sound of sizzling grease forced her attention back to what she was doing. She watched the chicken until it became a dark golden-brown and then took it out of the oil.

"Looks as good as it smells." Adam's deep voice behind her surprised Shiloh, making her jump and nearly fling a piece of hot chicken across the kitchen into the living room.

"Whoa, whoa…" Adam's face registered compassion, and Shiloh felt ridiculous for overreacting and for not paying better attention to her surroundings.

"Shiloh…" Adam stepped toward her. Slowly. As if he wasn't sure what she'd do.

He reached out both of his arms and folded them around her shoulders, gently, pulling her into his embrace.

Shiloh fought to hold her body stiff and resist the urge to melt into his strong arms—though the thought did cross her mind. She shoved it—and him—away as soon as it did, though. Hadn't she let Adam hurt her enough?

"Whatever's happening, we're going to figure it out."

She ignored his reassuring words. "Dinner's ready. Do you want to eat inside or outside? I have a table in the back I eat at sometimes."

"Outside's great."

"Okay." She nodded. "But the things I need to talk to you about will have to wait until after dinner, then. I'm not sure it's…safe…to discuss them out where anyone could hear."

"Sounds fine."

Shiloh led him to the back door, which he opened for her, always the gentleman.

"Wow." His admiring gaze moved over the landscape. "This is beautiful."

She looked around her personal oasis, trying to see it through his eyes. The wide wooden porch was simple, but the space was welcoming and comfortable. The yard below was well kept, draped by centuries-old live oaks. All of the small trees and brush on the five acres she owned had been cleared to afford her a good view of the entire area surrounding her house. Not only did she think it was gorgeous, it helped keep her safe and assured her that no one could get too close to the house without her seeing them.

"You did all this?"

Her cheeks warmed at his obvious approval, and she nodded. "Yeah. It's taken a while, but I like it this way." She shrugged.

"It's perfect."

They sat down at the table and fell easily into conversation. Half an hour or so passed, seeming like just a couple of minutes, and Shiloh noticed that the sky had darkened and that the musty scent of rain hung in the air.

Movement to her left caught her attention and Shiloh jerked her gaze to the trees at the back of her property. Had she seen something?

No. She was imagining things. She had to be.

Lightning cracked through the sky, illuminating the area, and this time Shiloh could clearly see the shape of a person darting from behind one oak tree to another.

She shoved her chair back from the table and took off toward where she'd last seen the figure. Somewhere in the distance, she heard Adam yell for her, but she ignored him.

Whoever this guy was, his first mistake had been killing four people in Savannah. His second was coming after her. She was going to catch him, going to end this tonight.

Her feet pounded the ground as rain began to soak the grass. She kept her eyes focused on where she'd seen the man last, which was how she saw him visibly startle when he saw her advancing toward him and take off running. She changed her course to follow him, pushed herself to run faster.

She was maybe thirty yards away from him by the time he neared the trees at the edge of her property. She couldn't let him get into the woods, or he'd be gone. She would have failed. Again.

Willing her body to find an even faster speed, she was so focused on her target that she failed to notice the slight indentation on the ground that caught her foot. Almost in slow motion she broke her stride and fell to the soaked ground. Through the pounding raindrops she watched the lone figure disappear into the shelter of the trees. She made a fist and hit the ground, splashing mud onto her clothes and face. Shiloh brushed some of it away, along with the tears she hadn't realized she was crying. Thunder clapped overhead, and Shiloh felt her hands start to shake.

Footsteps behind her seconds later made her jerk her head up, but it was only Adam.

"What were you thinking?" he demanded between puffs of breath. "Running off after someone alone like that?"

She stood, then said, "He was going to get away."

"Or he was going to lure you far enough away from help, from *me,* that he could attack you. Are you trying to kill me with all this worrying about you?"

"I'm an adult and a fully trained police officer. I can take care of myself."

"Why is it so hard for you to let someone else watch your back? People care about you. *I* care about you, and you're so intent on pushing me away."

She glared at him. "I never asked you to care."

"I can't help it, Shiloh." They stood face-to-face, rain pouring down, soaking both of them, making Shiloh's dark hair stick to the sides of her face.

Adam reached to brush it behind her ears but she swatted him away. He dropped his hand to his side. "Let's get inside before one of us gets struck by lightning."

As though on cue, lightning lit the sky again in twin jagged bolts. That and her already shaking hands were all the persuasion she needed to hurry back to the house. What was wrong with her? Why couldn't she get past this fear of storms? Weren't cops supposed to be fearless?

Once upon a time she would have agreed with the other Christians in her life, that she needed to give her fears to God and trust Him. She'd been a better Christian back in Savannah when Annie had been still alive. Shiloh turning her back on God when her cousin had died hadn't been intentional. She wouldn't even say she'd turned her back on Him. More like…it seemed He'd stopped being there. So she'd stopped expecting Him to be.

Another bolt of lightning and crash of thunder sent her running the final few yards to her back door. Once inside she shivered, rubbing her wet arms. "Thanks for coming."

"I'm not leaving yet." He had that stubborn glint in his eye that said he meant it.

Between losing the man who'd been watching her and the storm that still raged outside, she'd had the fight mostly drained from her. "Fine. I'm going to change. I'll be right back." She eyed his soaked clothes, trying not to notice the way his shirt clung to him. "I don't have anything that would fit…"

"I have a change of clothes in my car. If you don't mind, I'll run and get those and change in your spare bathroom."

She nodded. Minutes later she walked back into the living room to find Adam in dry clothes, sitting on the couch. The storm had grown more intense, and her hands weren't all that was shaking now. All of her was.

"Are you okay?"

Shiloh nodded but couldn't stop the shivering. She'd always hated storms but hadn't felt this sort of panic until recently. If she were to consult a shrink, the doctor would probably called it PTSD, since storms tended to give her flashbacks to the night she'd lost her cousin.

Please, please, Lord… To her surprise, Shiloh found herself praying. *Not tonight. Let me pull it together, at least in front of Adam.*

"Let's sit." Adam tugged her down onto the couch next to him, grabbed the fleece blanket she kept on the back of the couch and settled it around her.

Her defenses melted a little more at his kindness. *Remember he disapproves of your job, Shiloh. Besides, he's a pastor now, and you haven't been to church in who knows how long. You're completely wrong for each other.*

"Let's forget about what happened outside for a little while and talk about why you wanted me to come over."

Shiloh nodded, noting that her shivers had eased. Because of God? Or because Adam was such a calming influence? Both?

"It's about Annie…"

"And the warning on your car," Adam finished for her.

Shiloh paused as she tried to find the words. "You know Annie had been working on a big case before she was…" Shiloh began.

"Yeah. I didn't know many details, but I got the impression it was big."

"Three law-enforcement officials in the Savannah area had all been killed in the line of duty, and at first no one could figure out why. One was a port-authority worker. Another was a security guard at a historical-society building. The third was a Chatham County sheriff's deputy. Not exactly people who would have worked together, and there were no obvious reasons why they were killed on the job. No crimes had been obviously committed at any of the places where they worked. That's when Annie was assigned to the case."

Adam let out a whistle. "Attacking officers is serious. And not something other officers take lightly."

Shiloh nodded in agreement. "It's why Annie was so dedicated to this case, even more than she had ever been before. Anyway, through some investigation—I don't have all the details on that—she finally figured out the connection. These people are apparently some of those who believe there's buried pirate treasure off the Georgia coast. And they were sure enough that they were close to the location of the treasure that they were killing people who got in their way. That's why the officers had been killed. They were either reporting suspicious activities, or they had caught an intruder in the act at some point.

"Annie was being extremely careful." Shiloh felt a lump rise in her throat. "But she was willing to do anything to solve the case. Annie thought that if she could get to the treasure first, she could set a trap for the killers."

Shiloh took a deep breath, needing all the courage she possessed to confess the next part.

"After Annie was killed… You know how the press reported that the police had been working with a consultant on that case?"

He nodded slowly. "That's right—I remember. The department was furious that information went public. With Annie out of the way, her consultant would be the prime target of the killers, especially when the police stopped actively pursuing the case, since it had been so long without a lead."

"Exactly." Shiloh opened her mouth, closed it again, unable to say what she needed to. "But the thing is, since Annie believed the whole case was tied to pirate treasure, the consultant she needed was someone who knew the history of pirate treasure, legends and all of that."

Seconds passed in silence. Shiloh shivered again, this time not from the storm but from the reality of her next words.

"I was the consultant."

SEVEN

Lightning flashed outside, accompanied by a loud crash of thunder, but the drama of the storm was nothing compared to the feelings in his heart at that moment.

Shiloh was the consultant.

He sat in silence, feeling her eyes on him, knowing she was waiting for a response but unable to say anything as he processed what he knew. Gradually the puzzle pieces fell into place.

Shiloh was the consultant. Whoever had killed her cousin was after her.

The thought made his stomach churn, and he felt the hurt of not knowing, the fear for her, joined by anger. Forget the disagreement they'd had over women on the police force. At least they were trained for that kind of danger. When she'd agreed to be a consultant, Shiloh had been just a history professor. What had she been thinking?

Thoughts tumbled in Adam's head faster than he could sort them out. She hadn't told him. They'd been engaged, about to get married and merge two lives into one, and she hadn't told him.

She didn't trust him.

Adam looked up to meet her eyes, wishing he could believe that everything he saw revealed in them was true. She looked…regretful.

"I should have told you."

It was little more than a whisper, but it did do a little to ease Adam's tension. He exhaled. "This changes things."

"Yes."

"Those men who ran us off the road and vandalized your car—you think they're the same ones?" But Adam didn't know why he had asked the question. He'd seen the answer in that threatening note on her car window.

"Yes."

Not caring that they had more history to overcome than a textbook could hold, Adam did the only thing that made sense.

He wrapped his arms around her and held her. Tight.

He felt her relax in his embrace immediately. And unlike earlier in the kitchen, she didn't pull back. Instead she melted into him, leaving no doubt in his mind that he wasn't the only one wrestling with feelings that went far beyond friendship.

But they hadn't been able to make their relationship work under pressure last time. Everything had fallen apart when Annie had been killed. How would it be any different now, especially since he was aware of the fact that Shiloh's life was in danger?

No, there were too many things working against them, too many reasons why Adam and Shiloh together again was a bad idea.

This time Adam was the one who pulled away. As he did so, he saw Shiloh wipe a tear from her eye. Aside from the days following her cousin's death, he could count on one hand the number of times he'd seen Shiloh cry.

"What do we do now?"

Her voice wobbled, and his heart felt as though it could break. She was asking *him?* He wasn't law enforcement. Not even close. "The chief should know, Shiloh."

She shook her head. "Not yet. Someone's watching me—you know it as well as I do. And until I find out who's responsible, I can't trust anybody."

Adam stared at her in disbelief. "You think the chief might be involved with the killers?"

"No, absolutely not—but anything I say to him runs the risk of being overheard or of someone mentioning something in passing to the wrong person. Besides, there isn't anything the chief can do that I'm not already doing myself. No one knows this case better than I do. I know all of the background, even details that never made it into the case files because they were just speculations Annie and I made that weren't proven facts."

Adam considered that. "One question. If you've been working Annie's case for five years, why attack you now? I mean, what did you find that made you a target?"

Shiloh shrugged. "I have no idea." She raised her gaze to meet his. "I think it's entirely too coincidental that my life is quiet and then you come to town and suddenly it's chaos again."

"I don't know anything about this case."

"But maybe you coming back into my life gave them the impression that you did." Shiloh let out a sigh. "I don't know. I'm reaching here. But it's all I've got."

"Which is why you need another mind working on this. Talk to the chief."

She shook her head again. "It's too risky."

Several beats of silence passed as Adam searched his thoughts to see if there was anything else he could do that might help. "Do you think…? I mean, I don't know how, but do you think I can help?"

Hope flickered in her gaze. "I do. I was hoping you wouldn't mind."

Wouldn't mind. That was one way to put it. He'd give

anything to help and make all this go away—that was another way to put it.

"What do we need to do?"

"I need to walk back through the case in my mind and go over the details. You can be my sounding board and tell me if I'm overlooking anything."

"You mean, because you're so familiar with it."

Shiloh nodded. "Exactly."

"Why don't you tell me the basics of the case itself? Then we'll backtrack, and you can walk me through things. All I know is that it had something to do with pirates."

"Not just any pirates." A slight grin crept across Shiloh's face, and her eyes lit up like they did when she was talking about history or any good story. "Blackbeard himself."

He felt his eyebrows rise.

"Blackbeard was real," she continued.

Apparently, she'd gotten that kind of surprised reaction before.

"His real name was Edward Teach. He was probably English, though we're not positive, and we believe he spent a lot of time in the West Indies and on the East Coast of America, especially in the South. Georgia and the Carolinas seemed to be favorite spots for him, and there are so many stories, I couldn't tell you all of them in a year. Anyway, one of the reasons people are so fascinated by Blackbeard as a person and pirate is that he was kind of a classy pirate. A noble one, if you will. According to the stories, his crew worked willingly, and he hardly ever used violence against anyone, just intimidated them with his name, his ferocious-looking black beard and his reputation for being someone deserving of fear."

"So...the case?"

The look on her face betrayed her frustration.

Well, sue him; he'd hated history. Besides, she was in

danger, and he wanted to cut to the chase and figure out why. Not learn historical facts that may or may not be important. "Sorry."

"You have to understand the past before anything that's happened recently will make sense."

Wasn't that the truth about life? Suddenly, history didn't seem so useless after all. He nodded and told himself to focus. "Go on."

"His ship was named *Queen Anne's Revenge.* Historians think they may have found the remains of it off of North Carolina's coast. But anyway, from this ship he performed all his famous pirate deeds and amassed a huge amount of treasure. At least we speculate that it was huge. Some treasure was found in the wreck of what may have been his ship, but plenty is rumored to be buried all up and down the coast. This is where it ties in to the case.

"The killers are treasure hunters. That in and of itself isn't necessarily illegal, as long as they don't start digging on someone else's property or government lands. The problem came when they started killing people who got in their way. I don't know how Annie made the connection, but it must be right since that's what we were investigating when she was..." Shiloh swallowed hard.

"We'd done some research on Blackbeard, pinpointed possible locations for the treasure." Shiloh shook her head. "Annie and I searched all over the coast near Savannah. We went to Tybee Island, even kayaked over to Little Tybee Island. There was nothing there. I've been researching more and strategizing since then, but I haven't searched much yet."

"I like the plan of getting to the treasure first. Basically, you want to use it as a trap."

She nodded. "Exactly."

"So did you figure out where it might be hidden?"

There was that slow grin again.

Adam's heart pounded, whether from nerves, anticipation or downright attraction to the lady delivering the information, he wasn't sure.

"Ever heard of a place called Blackbeard Island?"

"No, but I'd say if I were Blackbeard, hiding my treasure at a place named for me would make all kinds of sense." He laughed as Shiloh rolled her eyes at his attempt at humor.

"It's one of the many barrier islands off the coast of Georgia." She hesitated. "It's an ideal hiding spot, and I should have gone before now, but…" A tinge of pink flooded her cheeks. "It's stupid that I've waited. But I didn't want to go alone."

"Sounds like something we should check out. I'm guessing there's no bridge."

She shook her head.

"Is there a ferry or something that goes to it?"

"Nope. You have to get to it by boat."

Adam's spirits sank. He should have known it wouldn't be this easy. He looked up at Shiloh and frowned at the smile in her expression. "What? You've already figured out a way to get us there?"

"I thought we'd take my boat."

He blinked. "You have a boat? Can I see it?"

"Sure." Shiloh stood and motioned for him to follow her as she led him to the garage. "Oh, and, Adam?" She tossed the words over her shoulder.

"Yeah?"

"Don't get any ideas—I'm driving."

He was still laughing when he drove home half an hour later.

He wasn't laughing, however, when he listened to the voice mail he'd gotten while he'd been at Shiloh's. He must not have heard his phone ring. It was Hal Smith, calling to comment on the amount of time that Adam had spent at Shiloh's house. The man didn't come right out and say it, but he seemed disturbed that Adam had spent so long there.

It made him uncomfortable to think the deacons had been watching him, knew where he'd had dinner, but he guessed that was why people referred to ministry life as the "fishbowl." He'd done nothing wrong, so he tried to push the entire issue out of his mind.

But it lingered there as he got ready for bed. There was no reason for his dinner with a friend to bother anyone. That didn't change the fact that it had. And Adam needed the good opinion of his deacons to keep his job, to minister to the church members and to make an impact on the community.

But Shiloh needed his help, too. As long as they were only friends, that couldn't affect the deacons or the congregation members at all. That was what Adam told himself as he laid his head on his pillow and closed his eyes. If only the feeling of uneasiness in his gut would listen.

Shiloh lay in bed hours later, unable to sleep but feeling lighter in her spirit than she had in weeks. Years, maybe. Telling Adam had been the right choice. She was sure.

She nestled her face deeper into her pillow as she thought about his arms around her, how tightly he'd held her as she had cried. It made the reasons she'd broken up with him seem unimportant, but they weren't…were they? When she'd made the decision to go into police training, she'd needed his support, his belief that she could do this. But when she'd counted on him to speak up, she'd only gotten silence.

And a thoroughly shattered heart.

Thunder rumbled low in the distance, the remnants of the summer storm that had chased them inside. The worst of it was over, though, so the gentle rumbles were almost comforting. They were reminders of how much better things had gotten, even in the past several hours. She and Adam finally had a plan, and that was doing wonders to ease her unsettledness.

Of course, she had no idea when they'd actually be able to act on their plan. The next few days would be busy for Adam. Word that he'd been accepted at the police department had gotten around town, and people were more willing to give this "newcomer" a chance. Adam's effort to win the trust of the townspeople impressed Shiloh. He genuinely cared about them and wanted to be a help to them. The way he lived out his faith in the love he showed to these people he barely knew…it was different than any pastor she'd known before. More passionate, more humble.

Adam had explained that he had several meetings scheduled but after that would do the best he could to be available during the hours she had off so they could work on the case. First she'd do more online research and make sure they both understood all the details that could figure into their physical search. Then they'd make a trip to Blackbeard Island.

Shiloh's heart raced. Blackbeard Island wasn't far. What if the people who were after her had set up a base for their operations here? They'd been lying low since the murders in Savannah, at least as far as she could tell. Maybe they'd just been working their way down the coast and had finally ended up here.

This sleepy coastal town of Treasure Point was Shiloh's safe haven, and she had embraced it over the past several years. Surely criminals would stick out like a sore thumb here. The men who had been harassing her must be living out of town somewhere and then coming to Treasure Point…but why?

Some of the pieces still felt as if they were missing, yet

Shiloh was having a hard time keeping her eyes open. It was either get up and make more coffee or worry about it tomorrow.

Before she could make a conscious decision, her eyes drifted shut, and Shiloh was powerless to stop sleep from overtaking her.

Her bedroom was bathed in darkness and moonlight when Shiloh's eyes snapped open. The night was still and quiet, and as far as she could tell, she'd been sleeping peacefully.

She lay there for another minute, but sleep wouldn't return. Instead the drowsiness of hours earlier had been replaced by an overwhelming feeling of alertness.

Something wasn't right.

She pushed back the covers and swung her legs over the side of the bed. She reached into the nightstand drawer and pulled out her Glock. She held it low at her side, praying she wouldn't have to use it. It wasn't unusual for her to wake up in the middle of the night; she hadn't slept well since she'd started this case five years ago, but this felt different.

She opened her bedroom door, wincing as it let out a low creak. Usually she appreciated the warning sound it gave—should someone try to break into her room while she was asleep. The noise was less appealing when it let an intruder know she was coming out.

The hallway was clear, nothing unusual or out of place. Shiloh continued to sweep the house as thoroughly as she would have done for a civilian. The guest bedroom and both bathrooms were clear. That was half of the house.

She entered the living room slowly, easing one foot in front of the other. The big room and its openness to the kitchen were two of the reasons she'd chosen this house. She loved how it looked. In the daylight. At night it was a vast span of unprotected square footage to cover. Perfect for someone hiding in the shadows to take a shot at her without her ever seeing them.

She scanned the room, pushing back her fear and inspecting every possible hiding place. Everything was as it should have been. Except...

Every sense on alert, she walked to her desk. Nothing was messy. In fact, everything was too tidy, and there were neat piles of papers where once there had been haphazard stacks. Her pulse quickened. She knew better than to keep anything important, professionally or personally, on or in the desk. It was the first place someone seeking information would check. But the fact that she suspected someone had been there looking...*in her house,* while she *slept*...

It scared her.

Shiloh flipped on a light, knowing she was done sleeping for the night, even if the clock on the wall read only 3:52 a.m. She was going to give this place another check. Better to be safe than sorry. She scanned the living room again, this time knowing she was looking for signs of anything being disturbed. She squinted a little and cocked her head.

Her bookshelf. Something didn't seem right there. Had they expected her to hide something important between the books? Maybe have one of those hollow books? She didn't, so she knew that search would have come up empty. She surveyed the books once more. She couldn't pinpoint what looked off about them but knew to trust her instincts. If she had harbored any doubt that someone had been here, she was unable to now.

She cleared the kitchen and laundry room for the second time. Walking back into the living room, alarmed at the knowledge that someone had been here, Shiloh realized something else was wrong. She paused; the outside noises she could usually hear—crickets, frogs—were louder than when she'd walked through this room before. And then she caught an odd hint of light out of the corner of her eye.

Moonlight spilled onto the floor of the entryway. The front door, which had been shut when she'd walked through the first time, stood wide open.

Someone had still been in her house while she'd been checking things. Watching her from somewhere in the darkness.

Shiloh shivered, overcome by a chill that went straight to her bones.

EIGHT

Adam knocked on Shiloh's door and then rubbed sweaty palms against his pants. He hadn't been to the police station yet today. One of his new congregation members had been rushed to the hospital. It had turned out to be nothing more than heartburn, but Adam had gone to visit anyway. Just to show his support. His dad had drilled into him from an early age the importance of being involved in his church members' lives, of being there for them.

Shiloh opened the door, then frowned. "Did we have plans tonight?" She glanced down at her workout pants and T-shirt. "Because if we did, I forgot."

"No, we didn't." Maybe coming over here hadn't been the best idea. "But I missed you today."

"I wondered where you were when I got to work this morning."

He heard a hint of vulnerability in that tone, as if maybe she'd missed him, too.

"Thought maybe you couldn't take the heat anymore."

"What? Like being run off the road and having the car I'm riding in trashed all within a week would scare me off?"

She laughed, but then her lighthearted expression gave way to something else. Something much more serious.

"Shiloh, what is it?" Adam asked.

"You'd better come in."

He followed her inside, discomfort growing as she glanced both ways in the front yard before shutting and locking the door with more force than was necessary.

"What?" He felt the urgency build in his tone.

She sank down into her desk chair. "I realized you didn't know yet."

"Didn't know what?"

"Someone broke into my place last night. Well, early this morning, really."

Heat surged through his veins. They'd been in her *home?* The previous attacks were in another category. On the surface, they looked more dangerous. But the knowledge that someone had managed to get into her house…

"Are you okay?" His arms ached to reach for her, but she'd chosen that desk chair on purpose, probably to keep him at a distance, judging from the way her arms were crossed protectively.

She gave a quick nod. "I'm fine. Physically. Emotionally, I can't decide if I'm mad or scared."

"It's okay to be both."

"Annie wouldn't have been scared. I don't think I ever saw her anything less than determined." Shiloh's shoulders sank a little. "I keep thinking I've come so far, but I'm still the nervous history teacher who refused to help at first when Annie needed it because I let fear control me. If I'd said yes to start with, maybe we'd have figured it out fast enough, and she wouldn't have…wouldn't be…"

He heard her sniff and thought she might cry again, but, instead, she blinked her eyes a few times, took a deep breath and sat up straighter. "I owe it to her to solve this. And I will."

"But you don't have to do it by yourself."

She nodded. "I know. You're right. That's why I finally told you."

"I wasn't talking about me. God is even more interested in justice than we are."

Shiloh snorted. "So I've heard. I'm not seeing it, though."

"You're only seeing part of the picture. Trust Him, Shiloh. He can help you sort through this."

She opened her mouth, maybe to make a snide remark, when their eyes met. "You…you really believe that, don't you?" She said the words so softly, so hesitantly, he had to strain to hear them.

"I do, Shiloh. And it has nothing to do with being a pastor."

She seemed to be considering his words. "I'll try to keep that in mind. But for now, I seem to be the only one working on this case."

"What about the department? Didn't they send someone to check out the…" He'd almost said *crime scene,* which a break-in technically was. But maybe that wasn't the best choice of words in relation to her home.

"The crime scene? I'm a big girl, Adam. I know what it is." She shook her head. "Yeah, they sent someone all right. He took pictures of my desk and bookshelf, which is all they seem to have disturbed, and went on his merry way. Oh, he also used a fingerprint kit circa 1980 but strangely enough wasn't able to find anything." She shook her head.

"He noted some scratch marks on the paint by the lock on the front door that show us that the intruder or intruders picked the lock to get in, but I could have guessed that anyway. Other than that…" Her voice trailed off.

"Not much of a crime-scene team. Or maybe I've just watched too much TV?"

"No, it's not much of one. It's just Officer Hitchcock, when he's not doing his patrol duties. If it was a murder or something, they'd call in a group from Savannah or Brunswick, but for stuff like this…"

"It falls through the cracks," he finished for her. "That's got to be frustrating. Why don't they do something?"

She shrugged. "Lack of interest or lack of funds, probably. It's not unusual for a town this size. Not that it makes it any less of a problem, in my opinion, but there's not a lot I can do about it." Shiloh sighed, then looked in his direction. "Why did you come again?"

"I thought you could use a break." And he was more convinced of that now. "Come with me."

"Where?"

He shrugged. "Anywhere. Out of this house. Maybe out of this town."

She looked down at the stacks of paper on her desk. "I should stay here and see if I can sort out what they were looking for. It's almost good they broke in. Everything they do gives us another clue, another chance to get closer to catching them."

"You realize you just said you're glad your house was broken into. You need a break. The case will wait, Shiloh. Let's go."

She opened her mouth to protest again and then closed it. "All right. Let me go change into jeans."

"You look fine like you are."

This time her laugh was genuine. "Thanks, Adam. I'll change anyway, though."

She returned in less than two minutes in a pair of blue jeans and a Georgia Bulldogs T-shirt.

"Okay, let's go."

They walked outside, and he watched her lock the door and test it.

He opened the door of the truck and motioned her inside. "Your carriage, m'lady."

She laughed. "I'd forgotten how you have that uncanny ability to make everything better."

"That's the goal. Now let's leave all of this behind us. Where should we go?"

She shrugged. "I don't know. Just drive."

He couldn't think of any words he'd rather hear at that moment. He climbed into the driver's seat, and they were out of Treasure Point's town limits within ten minutes. Adam almost thought he'd heard her breathe a sigh of relief when the lights of town were behind them as they drove along on a dark Georgia highway.

Neither one said anything for the first twenty minutes or so. True to her wishes, Adam just drove.

"I know where we're going." She finally broke the silence. "Turn left in about half a mile, at the big oak tree."

He did as she'd said. This road was dirt and bumped beneath the tires. Something about the rhythm of it calmed him, and he hoped it did the same for Shiloh. She'd been running for so many years—from memories, from him, from the men who had killed her cousin and even from God, too.

If he could get her to slow down, just for a couple of hours, maybe it would be enough to convince her to stop running.

"Pull off here." She motioned to what looked to be a field, shaded by a couple of large trees in the corner and then just open sky. "Drive on in. I know the owners. They don't mind."

He parked the truck in the middle of the field and looked to her for further direction. She grinned back at him as she reached for the door handle. "This is my favorite place to come and look at the stars."

He watched as she walked around to the back of the truck and climbed into the bed, situating herself with the cab for a backrest. "Come on." She motioned for him to join her.

He settled next to her, looking up at the inky-blue sky. "You're right. The stars are beautiful here."

"It's why I spent so much time at Tybee when I lived in Savannah. The city isn't that big, but the lights are still bright enough to dim the stars. It's even like that in Treasure Point. Here it's just pure, untouched darkness."

Adam drank in the brilliance of the stars, silently thanking God for His creativity and for the woman next to him. He reached for her hand, not sure how she'd respond, only to have her willingly thread their fingers together. He squeezed gently, feeling more content than he had in years.

Since she'd left.

"Hey, Adam?" Her voice broke into his thoughts.

"Hmm?"

"I still loved you, you know."

He was pretty sure his heart stopped beating. "What?"

"I still loved you, when I left. That wasn't why I ended things. I just wanted you to know."

Adam's thoughts battled within him. Part of him said it was time to demand some answers. He'd been left with a broken heart and a ring. No explanation. Nothing.

The other part of him said to wait. Let things happen this time without the past casting a shadow over what the future could be.

"I know I never told you. And I'm sorry for that. I left because…" She drew a breath.

He tightened his grip on her hand. "Shiloh, wait."

"Why?"

"It's in the past." His heart lightened as he said the words. "Maybe it's better if we leave it alone for now, just keep getting to know each other again without everything from back then crowding in. Sometime I want to know. I do. But maybe we should focus on right now. Let the past stay there."

In Shiloh's experience, the past never stayed there. It stalked her, haunted her thoughts and her dreams. It refused to give her a moment's peace.

But for Adam, she could try to ignore it. His hand tightened against hers and squeezed gently. He seemed to relax, and she found herself fully immersed in the present, being here with him under the stars like some kind of fairy tale.

What she'd said had been the truth. What she hadn't told him was that she wasn't sure if she ever had stopped loving him.

She worried they could never find their way back together with all the obstacles between them. But she wouldn't think about that tonight.

They sat in silence, maybe for an hour, maybe longer. For once Shiloh ignored the time, ignored what she *should* be doing and let herself just *be*.

Be still and know that I am God.

The words didn't come as an audible voice, or even a whisper, but more an impression on her heart. Could God truly still care about her? For the first time since she could remember, Shiloh felt at rest.

Maybe even at peace.

She knew the feeling wouldn't last. That as soon as she went back to real life, this feeling would evaporate like a fragile soap bubble, leaving no evidence that it had ever existed. But for now, she snuggled closer into Adam's side and closed her eyes.

It had been almost midnight when Adam had dropped her off. As much as she'd enjoyed their time together, she felt overwhelmed, and a few mornings later she was thankful that she still had a little while before she had to be at work so she could think things over. She needed to deal with some of the confusion swirling in her brain. Was Adam still interested in her? Did she even want him to be? She was the one who'd called off the relationship, and her reasons hadn't disappeared. If anything, they'd become more magnified.

Desperate to make sense of her thoughts, she drove down to the docks. Being by the water had always helped her think. She parked her car and walked toward the shore, taking a long breath of the warm, salty air and feeling her face relax into a smile.

Harry waved as she passed. "Morning, Officer Evans."

He was one of the fishermen always down at the docks readying for the day this early. She and Harry had had several conversations on mornings like this when Shiloh had come to sit on the docks. She'd even helped him with his nets one time, though the smell of fish combined with peppermint candy, which Harry always carried, had turned her stomach. Now she just waved and tried to keep her distance.

"Good luck fishing today," she called as she waved at him.

"Thank you." He nodded and went back to what he was doing but then paused. "Are you doing okay, Shiloh?"

The word *yes* was on the tip of her tongue when she realized that talking about this out loud might help. Maybe if she stayed far enough away from him to avoid too much of that smell in her nose?

"To be honest, not really. I'm confused about some things."

"You've come to the right place, then. I always think better out on the water."

"Life is just complicated," she stated.

Something flickered in his eyes. "I understand that." His

eyes fell to the dock, and he muttered, "Too well. But don't you worry—I'm sure you'll work out whatever's bothering you. You're a smart girl, Shiloh. I've always liked you."

She smiled. "Thanks, Harry. I hope I will." Shiloh glanced at her watch. She had to be at the station soon. If she wanted time alone, she had to hurry. "I guess I better go think some more and see if that helps."

"Have a good day." He waved again and this time fully refocused on his task.

She made her way along the dock, pausing to say hi to a few other fishermen she recognized. This was what she loved about a small town. Everyone knew everyone and liked them. She realized that sometimes newcomers were treated like outsiders, but she guessed the combination of her knowing the chief, showing up in town all alone with no family, had made the town accept her quickly. They'd adopted her as one of their own.

She walked down to the end of the dock and watched the waves lap against the weathered boards. There was something so constant about the ocean, even as it was so unpredictable. Its moods were almost beyond her understanding. Today it was relaxed, apathetic even.

She could have sat here for hours, but when she finally thought to check her watch, she had only five minutes to be at work. It took two to get there, but better to be a minute or so early than to be late.

She made it in plenty of time and sat attentively as the officer gave assignments for the day. She'd been tasked to drive Adam around, as she'd expected, and would be patrolling the area that included Widow Hamilton's house again. Her pulse skipped. Had the chief intended for her to investigate further?

"And, Officer Evans?" the lieutenant continued. "The chief wants you to talk to Mrs. Hamilton. Apparently, she's having problems with prowlers again." He smirked and several snickers followed from the other officers. The widow had become a joke around the department, but after finding the gold doubloon so close to the path that led to her estate, Shiloh was taking the old woman's stories more seriously.

"Yes, sir." Her heart pounded in anticipation of finding another clue. She met Adam outside, and they climbed into the car.

"How many days is that with this car? Three? Four? Is that some kind of record for you?" he teased as he buckled his seat belt.

"Ha-ha. Watch it, buddy. If I get tired of your constant ribbing, I may lose it and do something crazy like drive into a creek just to get you to be quiet."

She grinned at him, noticing that his eyes seemed to sparkle a little more than usual this morning. Because of their stargazing a few nights before?

"So what's on the schedule for the day?"

"We're patrolling near Widow Hamilton's place." Shiloh couldn't keep the excitement from her voice.

Was it her imagination, or did Adam tense in his seat? For now, she decided to ignore it. "After finding the gold doubloon, I'm more certain than ever that she isn't making things up. People probably really are prowling around her property. But why?" Shiloh frowned. "Maybe because it has so many private paths to the beach?"

"I can't believe he's sending you there knowing how much danger you've been in already."

Shiloh fought to keep her voice even. Were they really dealing with the helpless-woman thing again? He had no faith in her at all! "I'm the only one who will take her seriously. The chief knows that. I'm the best for this job, Adam."

Finally, the snarkiness she'd been fighting to keep out of her tone crept in again. "Even if I am a woman."

"Whoa." He held up his hands in fake surrender. "This has nothing to do with you not being capable. I think you're a great cop, Shiloh. I'm just worried about you. Can't a man worry about the woman he...?"

He trailed off, and Shiloh thought she detected a blush creeping up his face.

"Look, it makes me uncomfortable to think of putting you in someone's crosshairs. If you're right that someone or a group of someones has been on her property, they're probably up to no good."

Shiloh nodded, though the words he said didn't penetrate all the way to her heart. The other night might have been a nearly perfect fairy tale, but this morning they were back to the real world.

It was just as well, Shiloh tried to convince herself as she drove down the widow's narrow dirt driveway. She had a job to do. And she intended to do it well.

NINE

One of these days Adam was going to give up on trying to understand Shiloh. He studied her as she drove down the long dirt road to the widow's house. She seemed a little extra snappy this morning. That comment about being qualified in spite of being a woman had been especially pointed. Though he truly hadn't meant anything about her gender when he had told her that he was worried about her being in such direct danger. Maybe she was assuming things based on his...well, lack of support in the past.

When she'd told him in Savannah of her plan to become a cop, he hadn't known how to react. But she was starting to show him how well it suited her. It was almost as if she was made for the job, with the calm way she handled danger and kept her head in stressful situations. Even her reaction his first day in town, her choice to drive the car into Hamilton Creek rather than risk a crash, had been a smart decision. Shiloh thought on her feet well. She was a good cop.

Questions tumbled around in his head. Hadn't he given up a successful career in business to follow a calling? Did callings have to be to a specific *ministry?* Or could Shiloh really have been called by God to be a police officer?

In that case, he'd been wrong to give her anything less than his full support.

"Look, Shiloh…" he began slowly, afraid he'd say something that would make her mad again. "About the other night…"

"I don't want to talk about it."

She didn't take her eyes off the road, just stared straight ahead, giving far more attention to the driveway than it merited.

"But I wanted to ask you—"

"I said I don't want to talk about it."

He breathed out a sigh as he turned away from her, instead watching as an old white plantation house came into view. He let out a low whistle. "It's a wonder this thing is still standing."

"It's a beautiful piece of history," she defended.

"I didn't say it wasn't. But it's also showing signs of age."

"I suppose you're in the camp who would just tear this one down and build a new one?"

"No." He looked at her pointedly. "I think sometimes houses are worth restoring. If they can be restored safely."

She met his gaze. Hers softened ever so slightly. And then she nodded and turned away.

Somehow he was pretty sure neither one of them had been talking about old houses.

Shiloh parked the car and then strode to the door without waiting for Adam.

"Finally," Widow Hamilton snapped when she answered Shiloh's knock. "The chief says he sends someone every time I call, but no one ever stops to talk to me."

"I'm sorry about that, ma'am," Shiloh said in a calm voice, handling the situation with more ease than Adam would have been able to muster. "I'm here now. Tell me about what you've been noticing."

She bristled. "I will not tell you as you stand there on the porch in this heat. Come inside. I'll pour some tea and give you my report on the goings-on here." She nodded decisively, her mind made up. "And who is this nice young man?" She raised her eyebrows. "You don't have a uniform."

"I'm not an officer. I'm a chaplain and the new pastor in town. Adam Cole." He offered his hand, and she shook it with the grace of a genteel Southern woman.

"It's nice to meet you, Reverend Cole. Both of you, come inside now." She motioned them in, and they followed. "You may have a seat in the living room. I'll bring out the tea."

"Would you like me to help?" Shiloh offered.

Mrs. Hamilton's dark brows rose. "As though I'm too old to handle pouring some tea and serving it to my guests? Hardly, dear. But thank you. You may have a seat with this nice young man and keep him company."

Shiloh shrugged and sat down on one end of the sofa, perched on the edge. Adam took the other end, leaning back against the cushion.

He looked over at Shiloh. She was watching him. He shifted in his seat, trying to find a comfortable spot. As he spied Shiloh trying unsuccessfully to hold back a snicker, he realized she already knew what he'd just figured out. There was no comfortable spot on this couch.

Thankfully, they were soon distracted by Mrs. Hamilton's return with a tea tray.

"This is good tea," Adam contributed a minute later, feeling as if he should make some attempt to break the silence.

"Thank you, dear. Now, as for you…" Widow Hamilton directed her attention to Shiloh. "Since you've finally come to take my report, you should know that I've been hearing strange noises at night for several years now."

Just when Shiloh had gotten her hopes up again about a real lead. Mrs. Hamilton had been hearing noises for several *years?* Most likely a search of her attic would reveal an entire village of squirrels or something of the sort, which would account for the noises. Shiloh held back a groan.

"I wrote it off at first," she continued, "as paranoia. I called the police chief, just in case, but I wasn't terribly worried. The only real evidence I had was that things in the house, especially in my library, would be moved to places where I didn't put them. Almost like someone was looking for something."

"When did you first notice this?"

"Time goes by so fast now." Mrs. Hamilton tilted her head to the side. "Maybe five years ago?"

Chills crept down Shiloh's arms at the mention of the library and the time frame the woman had given. It was too coincidental that someone had searched both Shiloh's and the widow's book collections…but for what? Shiloh made a mental note to work on that question more later and focused back on the conversation.

The woman's voice softened as she continued. "So you can see I do have reason to believe there are prowlers on this property. I know what you people must think after so many false alarms. Maybe I was wrong to call at the slightest suspicion that something was out of the ordinary. But I know there's something going on here now. I heard noises a few nights ago, one of the nights it stormed. The next morning, I saw footprints."

"Why didn't you call the station?" Shiloh frowned—footprints would have been investigated more willingly than vague claims.

"Whoever I spoke to wouldn't even take a report. Can you help me?" The quaver in the elderly woman's voice was almost too much for Shiloh to take. She nodded slowly.

"Yes, Mrs. Hamilton, I think we can. I'll make sure anything you report from now on is given serious consideration." It was a promise she'd do her best to keep, even if she had to investigate every report herself. She recognized that haunted look in the widow's eyes, had seen it too many times in the mirror. Fear was beginning to rule the widow. Shiloh had hated it when that had happened in her own life; she'd do everything she could to keep it from happening to someone else. "And to start with, I'll investigate the premises myself today, with your permission, of course."

Mrs. Hamilton was already nodding, her mood considerably brighter in a matter of seconds. Funny what having someone believe in you could do.

"Of course. And please call me Mary. None of this 'Mrs. Hamilton' business or 'Mrs. Hamilton-Davis,' which is technically correct since Davis was my husband's name—people seemed to forget after he died that I had taken his name—or 'Widow Hamilton,' as rumor has it I'm known in town. I'm afraid this entire unsavory situation isn't going to go away anytime soon, so we're going to get to know each other very well."

"We'll do the best we can to solve this quickly, but I'll enjoy getting to know you in the meantime." Shiloh smiled. "Now, let's check out the library, since you'd mentioned problems there, and then we'll investigate some of the outside areas, if you don't mind." *Like those pathways to the coast,* she added silently.

"Certainly."

Shiloh followed Mary and turned to smile at Adam, who followed along behind her. He'd done an admirable job of letting her handle things. She'd have to thank him for that later.

They traveled down a narrow hallway lined with thin wood paneling painted in a faded white. Old houses like this fascinated Shiloh. She could tell elements had been updated over the centuries but guessed from the architecture that it had been built possibly as early as the mid-1700s, not long after Georgia had been founded as a colony and Savannah, its first city, had been built.

"Here we are." Mary motioned to a doorway on the right. Shiloh caught her breath as she entered, stepping carefully onto the Oriental rug that covered most of the antique hardwood floor.

The room resembled something out of a booklover's dream. Ceiling-high bookshelves lined three of the walls, and wingback chairs sat angled toward the grand stone fireplace positioned in the center of the remaining wall. A chandelier hung from the ceiling.

If Shiloh hadn't already known that the Hamiltons had come from money, she'd know it now. "This is beautiful."

Mary looked pleased. "I think so. My family has owned this house for several centuries. My love for it is part of the reason I'm eager for answers. I'd hate to leave it, but I'm starting to regret being here alone."

"I promise you," Shiloh reassured Mary, "I'll do the best I can to make sure everything settles down quickly."

"I appreciate that, dear. Now——" Mary moved to one of the shelves close to the fireplace "——they are arranged by category. This section," she said, then motioned to a set of shelves that included hundreds of books, "is the classical Christian section. It includes books that the Hamilton family considers staples of Christian literature." She pointed to a thick volume in the middle. "Dante's *Inferno,* some of John Donne's poetry, C. S. Lewis." She shrugged. "The classics span hundreds of years, but they include everything from poetry to religious allegory. It's a rather extensive collection, with at least one volume of every book of its type that the family considered a staple of such a collection."

Shiloh nodded as she took in the rows of books, most

of which she had at least heard of. She noted other famous names: Augustine. Milton.

"This is the section that had been…disturbed." A look of disquiet passed over the widow's face, and a soft frown shadowed her eyes. "I could never figure out if something was taken, or if things were only looked through. Either way, I haven't a clue as to why. They are valuable, to be certain, but there are more valuable things in the house." She sighed. "I'm rambling, aren't I, dear?"

"No, ma'am. Anything you can remember will help us," Shiloh said with a confidence she didn't feel. She had no more idea than Mary why someone would go through the books. Still, Shiloh's heart pounded as she wondered if the keys to finding the treasure and putting an end to this chapter of her life were or had been right in this room.

"I'll leave you two to look around." The widow cast one long gaze back at the library. "I used to love this room, but it doesn't feel quite right to me lately. And books I could have promised you I had have disappeared, right under my nose." She shook her head, shaking the doubt from her countenance. "I'll be in the living room if you need me."

Looking around the massive room, with no idea where to begin, Shiloh's words to the widow about getting things solved quickly repeated in her mind. She wondered if she'd made a promise she couldn't keep. This nightmare had dragged on five years so far. It was unlikely that it would disappear anytime soon.

Adam followed Shiloh out of the house and back into the heat about half an hour later, discouraged at how little they'd been able to find. But Shiloh still seemed bound and determined to find some kind of evidence before leaving the grounds. She led them to the edge of the woods and started down a trail lined with thick tangled grass and some cactus plants. He glanced at Shiloh's silhouette up ahead but then turned away. She looked good—better than good—but if he was smart, he'd keep his eyes on the ground and not appreciate her beauty too much.

He'd gotten a phone call that morning from one of the church deacons, asking why Adam had returned home so late the other night. At first Adam had thought the deacon was concerned that Adam's late night was connected to a church problem, so he'd tried to put the other man's mind at ease while being vague, but the deacon had finally come out and asked if Adam had been out so late with a woman. Integrity had forced him to admit he had, and the other man's disapproval had been evident as he'd warned Adam to be careful.

The implication that they didn't trust him had rankled him. Yes, he'd been with Shiloh. Yes, it had been something like a date. But nothing untoward had happened. They'd held hands; that was it. Yet the church leaders felt they needed a detailed update? He understood accountability, but this was taking it too far. Apparently, this small town had eyes watching everywhere.

Still, he wanted to succeed at this job. He knew he was called by God to be here. Besides, it was the first time in years that Adam felt as though his dad approved of him. Adam couldn't fail at his first church on his own, especially not in the first month.

Shiloh and Adam continued to wander through the woods for over an hour before she did an abrupt about-face and shook her head. "There's nothing here. We would have seen it by now if there was." She let out a sigh and wiped sweat from her forehead. "I'll keep checking back. I do believe her that something's going on, but without evidence..." She shrugged. "Let's go patrol the rest of our area."

"I think you're doing great, if that helps any."

"Am I?" She glanced around the thick brown forest and lowered her voice. "I've been chasing shadows for five years. Or trying. There had been no new leads, not one, since the night Annie was killed. I thought I'd lost my chance, that they'd gone underground, maybe found the treasure and disappeared, but now they're back. And I have to finish this. I have to."

He heard the desperation in her tone and reached for her, not knowing if it would help but hoping it would.

And she walked away. Story of his life.

She remained silent even after they'd gotten back in the car and started patrolling around the rest of the town.

"Hey, Shiloh?"

Still silence.

"I'm sorry about the whole situation. I wish there was something I could do."

"Thanks." She shook her head. "Sometimes I wonder if I just gave up, if maybe it would all go away."

Adam said nothing. She knew that wasn't true.

But two hours later—when she dropped him off at the station and went to finish her shift solo—she looked more defeated than he could ever remember seeing her.

Maybe she had given up after all.

At the end of her shift, Shiloh drove back to the station. She headed inside to clock out, had just stepped in the door when the chief grabbed her by the arm and hauled her into his office.

As soon as the door had shut behind them and they were alone, he said, "I know now, Shiloh." He folded his arms over his chest. "I made some calls this afternoon and got the answers you wouldn't give me. I know why you left Savannah. I know about your cousin's death and the case she was working on, and I know it's likely tied to whatever is going on now."

Shiloh felt her whole body tense in anticipation of the words she was sure to hear next—the ones dressing her down for not sharing this information herself.

"Tell me everything."

"It sounds like you know basically all you need to," she said with more confidence than she felt. He didn't seem to know that she was Annie's unnamed consultant…but Shiloh saw no reason to bring that up. Something inside stopped her.

The chief stared at her. "This isn't a game, Shiloh. These are real lives in danger. Not just yours, either, the entire town. Don't you care about that at all?"

"Of course I care." She heard the desperate tone in her voice. How could he doubt that, when this case was becoming all she could think about? She wanted to tell him everything, just as he had asked, so he could see how untrue that implication was.

She remained uncomfortable with the fact that she'd discussed pirate treasure with some of the guys at the department just days before the attacks against her had started. It could have been coincidence.

Adam, a tangible link to her past in Savannah, arriving in town was a much more logical, though no less confusing, explanation for the recent attacks. But Shiloh still hesitated to discuss her secrets with anyone in the department. Not until she knew if there was a mole, and if so, who it was.

She shook her head slowly, feeling the full weight of his disapproval as his face tightened into a frown.

"You don't have a choice, Shiloh. Tell me or your job is on the line."

She knew it was. Which would damage the case more— her getting killed or fired? Her brain hurt from thinking through all of the options. The best thing she could do was put it off.

"The reasons why I left Savannah aren't pleasant memories to revisit. I'm going to need a little time. For now, I'm going for a run on the coastal trail to clear my head. Maybe we'll talk when I'm done."

She walked out of the office, not waiting to hear his reply. She was so focused on the turmoil inside that she almost ran into Hazel, the department's secretary, on her way down the hall. Shiloh apologized and hurried outside. The last thing she needed was to give the chief enough time to come after her. He'd probably fire her on the spot for walking out the way she had, and it would be justified.

But she needed time to think.

Shiloh climbed into her car and drove down to the remote parking lot at the edge of Treasure Point. This was where the coastal trail began. She liked to run here because it wasn't crowded. Usually there would be no one else on the trail, just her and the ocean breeze. If that and running couldn't clear her thoughts, nothing could. She only hoped it would help today.

After parking the car, changing quickly in the public restroom, pulling on her running shoes and donning her service revolver once more, Shiloh started down the trail. Sunlight faded as she ran deeper into the trees, and the Spanish moss filtered the light further. Despite everything that still needed to be solved, Shiloh felt herself relaxing, felt the pieces of the puzzle that had been jumbled in her mind start to come closer to finding their places.

Two things needed her attention right now: finding the treasure so she could trap the criminals and working on a suspect list in her mind.

Shiloh and Annie had had no suspects, though they had been fairly certain—based on the nature of the injuries of the murder victims—that more than one person was involved and that they were male. Shiloh had believed them to be locals, because of the familiarity they'd shown with the Savannah area.

Shiloh rounded a corner, tensing slightly at the overhanging branches blocking her view of what was ahead. She relaxed upon seeing that the area was clear and kept running.

Now that the case had followed her to Treasure Point, she wondered if she should suspect one of the townspeople. It almost had to be someone local here, as well—outsiders stuck out in a town this small. But who could it be? One of her neighbors? One of the fishermen at the docks? Someone she saw at the grocery store?

Any random townsperson may as well be added to her mental list. She suspected them all equally—and with equally little probability. The killer had to have a solid knowledge of Blackbeard's history, but none of that information was hard to find—anyone with an internet connection and enough determination could figure it out.

The trickier part was figuring out how they'd learned about *her,* how they knew enough to be able to track her, follow her around without her spotting them. It had her suspecting that one of the assailants could be connected to the police department.

Several times she'd felt as though someone had been listening to a private conversation only to turn around and see no one out of place. Shiloh had always respected law enforcement, especially because her cousin and several other members of her extended family had been police officers.

But everything pointed to someone at the department being involved.

Not the chief. She trusted him. So who could it be? The idea of Hitchcock, or even Lieutenant Davies—much as he wasn't her favorite person—being involved made her almost sick to her stomach. Still, she had to acknowledge that it was a possibility.

If only the forensics from the crimes in Savannah had told them more. Even when they'd managed to get partial fingerprints at the crime scenes, the prints hadn't matched any on record. So either the murderers had successfully avoided arrest during an extended criminal career or Shiloh was searching for someone who'd become a criminal relatively recently. She was searching for a needle in a haystack.

Or a pirate treasure in hundreds of miles of coastline.

A snap in the woods alongside the jogging track jerked Shiloh to attention. She tried to tell herself it was probably a deer. Quickening her pace slightly, telling herself it was to push herself physically, not because she was scared, she rounded another bend in the trail.

A crack shattered the silence, and dust flew through the air less than ten feet from where Shiloh stood. Someone was shooting at her. She put her hand on her weapon. Instinct told her to seek cover from which she could return fire, but even after her scan of the area, she couldn't see where the shots were coming from exactly. To hide might put her directly in the shooter's sights. At least if she ran, she stood a chance.

She picked up her pace to a full sprint, making an effort to vary where she ran, darting left and right across the trail in an inconsistent pattern so the shooter wouldn't be able to get a clear shot off. Shiloh estimated she was half a mile from the end of the loop and the relative safety of her car. She ran faster, the tempo of her heartbeat pulsing through her head.

Minutes had passed since the first shot had been fired. She'd covered a lot of ground in that time. Unless the sniper was keeping the same pace as Shiloh, she should be safe. But the uneasy feeling prickling the back of her neck wouldn't let her relax. Shooter or not, someone was still watching.

The second crack sounded, and what felt like fire grazed her arm.

With everything she had left, Shiloh sprinted the remaining distance to the car and ran around behind it, putting it between herself and the trail where the shots had come from. She unholstered her weapon, then ducked into her car and reached for her radio to call for backup.

The crunch of tires on the gravel behind her made her swivel to face the new arrival, extending her arms and her gun in shooting position as she did.

Shiloh startled and lowered her gun when she realized it was another Treasure Point police car pulling into the lot. Still, she kept her finger near the trigger just in case.

Lieutenant Davies parked his car and stepped out. "You want to put that weapon away and tell me what you think you're doing?"

Shiloh's mind raced. Was it coincidence that he had shown up so soon after the shooting? There had been no more shots since he'd arrived. Could he have parked somewhere close and hidden in the woods to shoot her, then driven his car here to "discover" her body? Was he the one behind the attacks on her, trying to get her out of the way without blowing his cover?

The full sting of the graze on her arm and the anger at getting shot hit her all at once with more emotions than she could process.

"Someone shot at me." She said the words numbly, since he probably already knew. No, she was almost sure of it, since the gunshots had stopped as soon as he'd arrived.

It couldn't really be true.

But it had to be.

Any trace of a smile fell from Davies's face. "Did you radio it in?"

"I was about to when you showed up."

"Sure this isn't just something you're making up to get attention? Like when someone 'broke into your house' just to rearrange your bookshelf?"

She tensed. "Someone was there."

"There was no evidence. Only your word."

She wanted to scream. "Let me radio the chief."

"You should do that. Heard you had words with him earlier."

More pieces fell into place. Had Davies been eavesdropping? Her trip here to run had been spur of the moment. She'd only mentioned it that once in the chief's office. For someone to have been waiting here to shoot her, they would have had to overhear her and react immediately. If anyone had the opportunity to do it, it would be this man in front of her.

"Stop looking at me like that and radio the chief. He sent me over here to check on you and tell you he wanted to talk to you again when you were done with your run."

"How did you know about my run?" she shot back with suspicion coloring her tone.

"The chief told me." He glanced around, taking in the sunny day and peaceful scene. "You're sure someone was shooting?"

She angled her injured arm toward him. "Does it look like I'm making it up?"

He took in the red streak on her arm and raised his eyebrows. "Could be a scratch from anything."

"It's a bullet-graze mark," she ground out between her closed teeth. "You didn't hear the shots?"

"Can't say that I did."

Suspicion weighing like blocks of ice on her soul, Shi-

loh reached for the radio and called in the incident. Since
there had been no more shots, she took a seat in her car to
wait, deciding she'd prefer not to talk to the other officer
at the moment.

Someone had shot her. Someone who'd known her plans
to go for a run. And though she'd only suspected it until
now, she now knew someone at the police department was
involved. And unfortunately, she was afraid she knew exactly who it was. She hated the idea of a dirty cop. She
hated even more the fact that Lieutenant Davies was well
respected in the department. Unless she had solid proof
that he was involved, no one, not even the chief, would believe a word she said.

Adam had been in his church office staring at a commentary for over an hour and still saw only words blurred
together. He was too distracted by the look of defeat he'd
seen on Shiloh's face earlier in the day.

With a sigh and a shake of his head, he shut the book.
His inability to focus wasn't likely to resolve itself anytime soon.

A knock at his open door made him jerk his head up.

"Hello, Pastor." Winston Howell, one of the older men
at the church, stood in the doorway wearing his trademark
overalls. "I was in the area, picking up some parts for a
truck I'm fixing, and wanted to drop by to talk to you about
Sunday's sermon."

Sunday. Adam had been moderately happy with the message he'd gotten across but felt some of his points could
have been better articulated. Half of his mind had been
with Shiloh, stressing over the break-in at her house. Anxiety swirled in his stomach as he waited for what the man
would say.

Winston stuck out his hand. "You're a real man of God,

Pastor Cole. I can tell that from the way you preached His word. Thank you for the job you're doing here."

Adam shook his hand, unable for a moment to find the words to respond. Finally, he managed a thank-you. After the insinuations from one of his deacons that Adam's propriety couldn't be trusted, this man's words lifted his spirit. Maybe there was hope that he could make an impact on this community after all.

And make his father proud in the process.

"Thank you." He echoed the words again. "I appreciate the encouragement."

Winston nodded in his easygoing way and stepped out of the office. "I won't keep you, Pastor. I know you have work to do. I just felt led to say something."

"And I'm glad you did."

As he listened to the man's muffled footsteps travel down the hallway, Adam looked back down at the commentary and opened it again. This time thoughts flowed in his mind as he read, and he jotted notes down on the legal pad beside him, eager to see another week's sermon taking shape.

The next moment he looked up at his clock, it was later than he had expected. As he sat there, concern for Shiloh invaded his mind, and Adam felt a clear compulsion to find her. He closed his commentary and drove to her house. After several minutes of standing on her porch and ringing her doorbell, his worry had intensified. He pulled out his cell phone, wondering why he hadn't thought to call her in the first place. He dialed her number. No answer. He drove to the police station, noticing there were fewer cars in the lot than usual—implying they were out on calls. Or maybe one big call. He hurried inside as fast as he could.

The atmosphere told him immediately that something wasn't right. It was a combination of frenetic energy and eerie silence.

"Reverend Cole." The secretary, Hazel White, her face lined with stress, let out a sigh of relief. "I couldn't find the paperwork with your cell phone number anywhere, but I knew they'd want you at the scene. Do you need directions?"

A lump gathered in his throat and he felt his chest physically tighten. "Scene?"

The secretary blinked wide eyes. "You haven't heard? It's one of the officers. Someone shot her while she was running on the marsh trail."

He was pretty sure he was going to throw up. "Which officer?"

Several beats of silence passed, and he could see the secretary hesitate as his emotions played across his face.

"The one you've been riding with. Officer Evans."

He ran out of the building. Wished he'd listened to the urge to find Shiloh sooner. And prayed he wasn't too late.

TEN

"I'm fine," Shiloh repeated—for what had to be the tenth time—to the EMT working on her arm. No one listened, which came as no surprise since they hadn't listened so far.

"What happened?" The chief's gruff voice—the very thing that had angered her so much not an hour ago and had caused her to go for a run on this trail to calm down—seemed comforting and familiar now.

"I rounded the corner there—" She motioned with her good arm, which apparently still bothered the EMTs since one of them grunted and told her to be still. "And shots were fired. Two. The first was low and kicked up the dirt maybe five to seven feet away from me. The second grazed my arm. Whoever we're looking for is not the best shot."

"Shiloh, it's becoming clear that these aren't idle threats. Someone is trying to kill you."

She snorted, still feeling the adrenaline rushing through her. "They're not doing a very good job."

The glance the chief shot her was less than amused.

Shiloh shrugged apologetically. "Look. I thought about what you said. And while I still don't love the idea…" She was ready to tell him the rest of what had happened. But as she glanced at the horde of people around her, she realized now wasn't the time to communicate that to the chief.

He nodded, apparently having seen her thoughts in her eyes. "Come to my office when they're done with you. I'm going to go look around, give Hitchcock another set of eyes."

Ah, their crime-scene team of one. Once again her town's need for a real crime-scene team was glaringly apparent. Nothing against Hitchcock. But there was only one of him, and his training didn't qualify him as an expert in forensics. Hopefully, he'd be savvy enough not to waste the gift they'd been given here now that their criminals had gone this far.

Shiloh just nodded. "See you later, Chief." She sat still as the medical people continued to clean her wound. It seemed to be taking a long time, particularly when it was nothing more than a scratch, but when she'd suggested initially that someone let her have a bandage and call it good, the reaction hadn't been favorable.

"Where is she?"

What had been a thunder of different voices in the background gave way to one very clear, panicked voice that she didn't have to work to recognize.

"Adam! I'm over here!"

She thought she saw the top of his head as he ducked around people and made his way to her. Finally, there he was.

"Are you okay?" His eyes flickered to her arm. "No. You're not."

His face was paler than she'd ever seen it, and his eyes looked softer, less guarded than they had since he had come to Treasure Point. In that instant, it would've been easy to believe that the past five years had never happened, that they were still engaged. That maybe, just maybe, he still loved her.

"I'm fine."

His eyes searched hers, and Shiloh wasn't sure if it was

the emotion of the moment or something else, but she wanted nothing more than to lean forward and touch her lips to his.

If they hadn't been surrounded by a crowd of people, she probably would have done it. For the first time in the past forty-five minutes, she was a little thankful for the attentive group around her.

"We're all done here, Officer Evans. Make sure you keep that clean. Come in next week for a checkup."

She nodded. It wasn't the first time she'd been grazed by a bullet—though the last time she'd simply been in the wrong place at the wrong time. This time the shot had been meant for her. "I will. Thanks. I know I'm not the best patient."

The EMT had no comment. Or if he did, he kept it to himself.

Just like that, the crowds of people wandered away, apparently having decided that nothing too exciting was going on. A few officers were still around, but they'd spread out to canvass the area. Right here, it was just Shiloh and Adam.

And her ridiculous urge to kiss him.

He reached for her hand and gently rubbed her fingers with his thumb. "When they told me you'd been shot…" His voice, deeper than usual, trailed off. "I'd been worrying about you for a little while before I left the office, wondering if I'd done enough to keep you safe."

"I'm fine." How many times would she need that line today?

Adam gripped her hand more firmly. "We're going to end this. Soon. We need to figure out what happened."

"Don't make promises we both know you can't keep, Adam. I have to go talk to the chief. I'll talk to you later."

"I am not taking time off." If Shiloh'd had any idea that this was what the chief had wanted to talk about, she'd have refused to come to his office, even at risk of losing her job.

As it was, she risked losing it anyway. Forced leave? That wasn't something that happened to good cops. That was the stuff of internal-affairs investigations, something that happened to people who had messed up.

She'd done nothing wrong, besides attract trouble, and that was hardly her fault.

The chief's expression didn't change. "Just a few days, Shiloh. Go on vacation. Stay home and read a book. I just think you should lie low and give us some time to look into this."

"Us?" That fanned the embers of indignation more than anything else had. "*Us* is the department. I'm part of that. You'd put me on leave, make me take vacation, whatever it is you're calling it, when we're already short staffed?"

"Let's give it a few days, and maybe you can come back and work on it again. But you and I both know you're not just an officer here, Shiloh. You're a victim, and from the research I did, it's plain to see that these threats against you could be connected to what happened to your cousin in Savannah." He leveled her with a glance. "Though I still don't know why they'd be interested in you, since you were a civilian in Savannah."

Shiloh was quiet. She'd come into this office ready to tell him everything about the case, but if he was taking her off duty temporarily because she was too close to the situation, there was no way he'd let her return to work if he knew the whole story. Which left only one option.

He couldn't know.

"Take those days off." His tone left no room for argument. "I'll put you back on the shift schedule for next week."

"It's Tuesday." Shiloh blinked. "Three days off?"

"Five days with the weekend."

Never had she wanted to pitch a screaming-toddler-type tantrum so badly. "I'll see you Monday, then."

"And not before."

She stood and walked to the door. As she reached for it, she paused. "Chief? Do you trust Lieutenant Davies?"

He looked bewildered by the question but answered without hesitation. "Absolutely. One hundred percent."

Just what she was afraid of. Though her suspicions pointed to Davies, it would be her word against his. The chief trusted them both, but the lieutenant outranked her. That might carry some weight. Besides, the chief was irritated with her for keeping things from him.

"Thanks."

Shiloh walked out of the office and closed the door behind her. She'd call Adam and see if he'd be willing to start their unofficial search first thing in the morning.

"So what exactly are we looking for?" Adam called to Shiloh, who was in the kitchen making coffee.

"Anything linking Blackbeard and Treasure Point. I have a feeling it's Blackbeard Island, but the island is going to take some effort for us to access and search, so we should be relatively sure before we go to the trouble."

"Got it." Adam opened his laptop. He'd initially suggested they meet at her house, but she'd pointed out that it was more likely their online steps could be traced there, especially since someone was already watching Shiloh.

So his house it was. It had taken the dog all of ten seconds to declare undying allegiance to Shiloh and to start following her around as if she'd invented Milk-Bone treats. Tux had good taste; Adam would give him that.

"I'll be right in as soon as I figure out how to use your machine. My brain doesn't work right without coffee."

Adam searched for Blackbeard Island. One site had nothing to do with the actual place but with some kind of animated game. That wasn't useful. The next hit looked as if it had been made by a kid for a class project. That wasn't what Adam was looking for, either.

So far he was zero for two.

The third was the official site for the U.S. Fish and Wildlife Service. Definitely legit. Whether it held any important information would be a different story.

He skimmed the first paragraph, which detailed some of the island's history and how the navy had originally owned it. Finally, he got to the part that interested him—the part that mentioned Blackbeard and a possible treasure. Unfortunately, it told him only what he already knew. He returned to the search-results page.

Another site was a treasure hunter's forum. Adam read through some of the posts. One mentioned several different treasures supposedly hidden in Georgia, including one by Blackbeard. Another poster insisted that Blackbeard Island hid nothing and discouraged people from trying anything, since its status as a wildlife refuge made treasure hunting there illegal. Yet another commenter, who sounded as if he might admire pirates a little too much, insisted that Blackbeard's treasure did exist and could be hidden anywhere along the Georgia coast.

Adam pulled up a Georgia map and noted for the first time how jagged and pocketed the coastline was. And much of it was well connected to rivers that went even farther inland. None of that helped narrow down anything.

So Blackbeard Island looked like the best option. At least it gave them a place to start other than searching the hundreds of square miles where Blackbeard could have hidden his treasure.

Adam smelled the coffee brewing—thankfully. He was

already fighting the urge to pinch himself to see if he was really awake and aware and searching for pirate gold.

The things a man would do for a woman.

"Coffee's almost done." Shiloh walked in and sat down beside him, brushing a strand of hair behind her ear as she did so. "What have you found out?"

He summarized for her, and she nodded as if she'd heard it all before, which made sense since she'd probably learned all that in college.

Adam continued. "The thing that seems to point to Black-beard Island is its proximity to both Savannah and Treasure Point. You were thinking the men were using each of the towns as basically a base to start their search from, right?"

She nodded. "Exactly. I think they started in Savannah because it's a big city. It's easier for strangers to blend in. Then when everything escalated in Savannah, I think they moved here."

"Because it was the next best choice." Something about that didn't sit right with Adam. "Why not one of the bigger coastal towns? Darien, maybe?" The nearby town was larger than Treasure Point and just south.

That thought seemed to trouble Shiloh, too, but in only a moment her expression cleared. "We're almost due west of Blackbeard Island here. Treasure Point is smaller than Darien, but not by much. Maybe the proximity made it worth it."

Her explanation was logical enough. "So we're pretty set on Blackbeard Island. Want to check it out tomorrow?"

"Yes. So maybe today we should research possible hiding spots on the island? See if we can find any information online about places that have been searched already?"

He nodded and within five minutes had two maps of the island printed, one for each of them. "I thought we'd mark what we find separately and then compare."

Shiloh's appreciative smile made his time off from work more than worth it. "Thanks, Adam."

"You're welcome." He forced his thoughts to the map and the research waiting to be done. Seeing her whole face light up meant too much to him. He'd do almost anything, sacrifice almost anything, to see her look at him like that.

And it scared him half to death. Hadn't she left once already with no warning? What if he turned his life upside down for her and she left again?

Worse yet, what if he did everything he could to help her solve this case and she ended up dead? Like Annie. Like his mom.

He'd said he wanted to leave the past behind them. But he had to know why she'd left. Now all he had to do was get up the guts to ask. Adam glanced over where she sat working on her computer. He'd ask when she was done with what she was doing.

Minutes later, Adam heard Shiloh slam her computer shut.

This was his chance.

Shiloh looked over at Adam to find him staring at her. "What?" she asked.

"Shiloh…"

His intense gaze bored into her.

"I changed my mind. I need to know—why did you leave?"

Words warred in her mind as she struggled to articulate all the confusion and anger she'd felt when she had left. "I felt…betrayed by you. You said it was Annie's fault she was killed. That women shouldn't do any kind of dangerous work."

He said nothing.

She continued. "I knew already that following in her

footsteps and finishing what she'd started was the least I could do for her. And you made it abundantly clear that you wouldn't support that."

Or had he? Technically, his father, her pastor at the time, had been the one to insist that Christianity didn't permit women to hold dangerous jobs. But Adam certainly hadn't argued, and when Shiloh had brought it up, he'd backed his dad's opinions.

It had hurt then, to her very core. And it hurt now to remember. She tried to edge away from him on the couch only to realize she had no room to move. She was essentially pinned between the arm of the sofa and Adam.

She sneaked a glance at him. Adam's emotions were written clearly across his face. He looked...devastated.

"We lost five years together because of a difference of opinion about the best careers for women?"

Any emotion that had stirred in her heart to see him so broken was crushed with that question. A difference of opinion? "This was more than a friendly disagreement. You and your father all but told me Annie had sinned by becoming a police officer in the first place. I knew I was about to do the same thing and that you'd want no part of it."

"I never said it was a sin, Shiloh."

"Well, your father sure did, and you backed him up. So either you did agree with him or you were so concerned with impressing him that you were more interested in supporting him than your fiancée who you supposedly loved."

The words seemed to slap him in the face.

"'Supposedly'? I did love you, Shiloh. I wanted to give you everything. We were to be married. You are the one who left. You. Not me."

"I left because you didn't support what I wanted to do with my life. I knew then, Adam, *knew* that becoming a police officer wasn't just a crazy idea to try to honor my cousin. I knew I would be good at it, that God wanted me to do it. And I knew you wouldn't accept that."

"You couldn't have known it because you never gave me a chance."

Was that true? She'd been so sure, but looking into his eyes now, which mirrored her own heartbreak and looked as though they hurt along with her, she didn't know. Shiloh felt some of the anger leave her, and her shoulders fell. She blinked stinging tears from her eyes and pushed herself up from the sofa. "I think it's time for me to go."

"Shiloh…" Adam stood but Shiloh had already turned away and started for the door.

Then a hand grabbed her shoulder, and in one motion Adam spun her to face him, his palms on her upper arms, and kissed her.

Shiloh tensed and almost pulled away, but he drew her in, and before she knew it she was kissing him back, deepening the kiss.

This was perfect. Wonderful. The feel of his lips on hers made her dream of the future they could have—transported her back to the past and the relationship they'd had then.

She watched a slide show of mental pictures of their relationship flash across her mind until she came to the night she'd left Savannah.

Shiloh broke the kiss, pushed herself out of Adam's arms, far enough that he couldn't reach her.

"We shouldn't have done that." She folded her arms over her chest, took a deep breath to slow the pounding of her heart.

Adam opened his mouth to protest and then shook his head. "You're right."

She'd expected him to tell her that she was wrong. To convince her to give their relationship another chance. Then again, hadn't he let her walk out of his life before without the slightest attempt to get her back?

Shiloh shook her head as though to clear the confusion from her mind. Not that she wanted him to try to get her back. No, if anything the kiss had proved that her feelings for him were stronger than she wanted to admit. He'd hurt her once by not supporting her, not believing in her abilities. She wasn't going to give him the chance to do it again.

ELEVEN

Shiloh had half expected it to be raining today, since they'd planned to go to Blackbeard Island, yet the sky above was cloudless blue. She loaded her car with the last of the supplies she'd packed for the day and double-checked the boat trailer to make sure she had everything hooked up correctly.

She heard a truck pulling in and glanced up from her task just to make sure it was indeed Adam. Almost unconsciously she rubbed her shoulder where the bullet had grazed her the other day.

"Good morning," Adam called as he walked across her driveway.

"Good morning."

"Ready to wrap this up?"

Her stomach fluttered at the possibility that they might be hours away from her ending this nightmare forever. Hours away from finally seeing justice done for her cousin's death.

"*Ready* is an understatement." She checked the gas level in the boat one more time. It was full, almost brimming over. That should be plenty to get them from the public boat launch out to Blackbeard Island and back.

"Do we have enough gas?"

She slammed the tank shut. "Yep. Checked it twice."

They made the drive to the boat launch without much

talking. Shiloh was sipping the coffee she'd brewed, and Adam appeared so deep in thought about something that she hated to interrupt him.

"So do you get out on the water much?" he finally asked.

"Not as much as I'd like," she confessed. "I don't have the time."

"You should make more time in your life to have fun. I know things are crazy right now. But you should be able to really live life and enjoy it, you know?"

He had a point. Even though she'd escaped death in Savannah—unlike her cousin—Shiloh hadn't really truly lived since then. She had been held captive by...she'd like to call it common sense. Or being cautious. But it was fear.

Would she ever escape it? She didn't know.

After launching, Shiloh parked the car and then waded back through several feet of water to climb into the boat with Adam.

"I still think you should have let me do that part."

Bless his chivalrous heart. "Have you ever launched a boat before?"

His silence was more than an adequate answer.

She laughed. "Thanks for the thought."

She eased the boat through the narrower parts of the marsh then went into a faster gear until the salty air whipped through her hair. She found her face relaxing into a grin. One day, when she had more time, she'd do this every day. Or at least the ones that she had off from work.

"This is awesome!" Adam shouted over the noise of the motor and the waves.

If she could ignore that paranoid part of herself that said they could possibly be heading straight for danger, this would be the perfect day. Out on her boat, the sun shining down, making the water glisten, with Adam by her side.

With sudden clarity she saw how lonely the past few

years had been and knew that it wasn't the boat ride or the beautiful day that made her feel so content. It was being with Adam.

Shiloh slowed the boat again as open water turned back to marshes and creeks, which she'd have to navigate through to reach the island.

"It's unreal out here. It looks different than anything I've ever seen," Adam remarked.

Shiloh looked around, trying to see it through his eyes. She hadn't been to Blackbeard Island, but she'd spent enough time on Georgia's coast around other barrier islands that the scenery, while breathtaking, seemed familiar to her. The wide creek they'd entered separated Blackbeard Island from Sapelo Island. Blackbeard was the one closest to the open sea, which was why it had the remarkable beaches she was looking forward to seeing in person.

As she turned the boat around a sharp corner, following directions on a map of the island Adam had printed, she could see why this place made a likely hiding spot for pirate treasure. There were so many little creeks running off of the main creeks where gold could have been buried, not to mention the potential hiding places on the island itself. From this angle she could see the sand that met the water's edge, and then tall pine trees standing guard like sentries over what was now a wildlife refuge, but could have once been, and probably was, one of the frequent haunts of the most famous pirate in American history.

It gave her chills to think of the stories this place could tell if islands could talk.

Shiloh piloted the boat to the designated dock where she and Adam anchored.

"This is it?" He looked around, his features edged with confusion.

"Did you expect something different?"

"Not too different. Maybe just a little more…a little more."

She could see what he meant. There was no large visitors' center, no hordes of tourists flocking. Just a docking space, really. And a sign denoting it as a wildlife preserve.

"Let's hit the trails." Shiloh finished tying off the boat and motioned to her backpack, which was still in the boat with Adam. "Could you hand me my pack, please?"

Adam grunted as he lifted it, and his brows rose in surprise. "Is there anything you *didn't* pack in this thing?"

Shiloh did her best to look indignant. "It's just things I thought we might need…food, a first-aid kit, extra water, a camera to document anything we find." Her back would probably be killing her by the end of the day, but it would be worth it. Shiloh felt those excitement shivers again as she surveyed the area, trying to decide where they should start. "I think we should take the wilderness trails first. They form a loop, and then we can go back to the beach trails and up to the north end of the island."

Adam looked over her shoulder at the map and nodded. "Sounds like the best plan. Want me to carry that?" He motioned toward her pack.

She shook her head. "Thanks, but I've got it."

"At least put something back in the boat. Is there anything you can take out?"

She thought over the list again and shook her head.

"How many 'extra' bottles of water did you bring? I have one here for me." He lifted it in the air as if to emphasize his point.

She'd packed five for each of them, just to be on the safe side. Wordlessly, she swung the backpack off and handed some of the bottles to Adam along with a key to her boat's storage compartment.

"If you use this key to unlock it, you can lift the lid on

that seat there—" she motioned "—and I guess we can leave these here."

"Sounds good." He climbed into the boat and did as she'd asked. Shiloh put the backpack on again. Much better.

After only minutes of walking on the wilderness trail, Shiloh got the eerie feeling she had literally stepped back in time. It was a sunny day, and there were no doubt more people on the island, because she'd seen several kayaks at the dock. But out here it was impossible to feel that way. The gravelly dirt pathway was lined with saw palmettos that were as tall as she was, and the live-oak trees that grew along the track had large branches that overhung the trail and dripped Spanish moss down.

The swordlike leaves of the palmetto and the gray Spanish moss dimmed the sunlight and made this path seem much, much darker than the rest of the island. Shiloh shifted the backpack a little and tried to reason away the uneasiness that had stolen her earlier sense of peace and contentment.

Was she scaring herself and allowing the hostile-looking environment to play tricks on her? Or was her subconscious picking up on a threat and warning her to stay alert?

She glanced behind her and scanned the entire area. Nothing but Adam and utter wilderness. She smiled at him, hoping her unease wasn't clear in her eyes, and turned back around.

Yeah, she could definitely see pirates, or any other kind of criminal, being at home here.

"So how should we be searching?" Adam asked in a low voice, close to her ear. She appreciated how softly he spoke, just in case trouble had followed them here. Or in case they'd followed trouble. In either situation, it was best that they be moderately inconspicuous, like two hikers out for the day, for as long as possible.

She shrugged. She hadn't gotten quite that far in her

plans. Maybe she should have borrowed a metal detector from someone in Treasure Point. Of course, that would have raised questions. Besides, treasure hunting was illegal on the island. Shiloh was ignoring that by telling herself they weren't really *treasure* hunting. They were hunting the treasure hunters themselves. Just in case, she'd tucked her badge and gun in the backpack. She'd still get in trouble, especially if they called the chief and discovered this wasn't official business, but hopefully, her credentials would keep her from paying an exorbitant fine or landing in jail.

"Just keep your eyes open," she finally whispered to Adam.

They pressed on deeper into the woods, Shiloh still feeling as if every step was taking her further from her comfort zone. A warm breeze rustled through the trees just as the sky darkened, and they lost even more light. What was it about these woods? Everywhere else she'd ever been in coastal Georgia had felt like home to her.

Careful inspection of the trail and any wildlife paths shooting from it had revealed nothing. If the treasure was hidden in these woods, it was probably undiscoverable, by Shiloh or anyone else. She couldn't decide if that made her feel relieved or frustrated. On one hand, finding the treasure was her best shot at locating the criminals. On the other, if she couldn't find it, that meant they probably hadn't, either. After the murders they'd committed, it just seemed wrong to think that they might get what they wanted.

Just when Shiloh thought they were lost in these woods forever, the light grew brighter and she realized she could see sandy beaches and the ocean up ahead. "I guess we'll try another trail."

"Sounds good to me."

They took the north trail. Just the one trail they'd hiked

so far had taken several hours, and Shiloh had already de-cided that if they were here after sunset, she'd want to be on the beach, not on the trail that bordered the wilderness area.

Especially since the map indicated it led to Crematorium Road. She didn't even want to ponder what that meant.

"Is it safe to talk?" Adam asked once they were well on the new trail.

Shiloh shrugged. "I suppose, a little. What about?"

"If you have any ideas about…who. In Treasure Point, I mean."

She hated the thought that someone she knew might want her dead, but given the way her conversations got back to the criminals, the conclusion was inescapable. No one she'd talked to had reported seeing strangers in town lately. Either they'd done a phenomenal job lying low or it was one of the people in town.

Maybe it was because she'd made Treasure Point into a modern-day Mayberry in her head, but that thought hit her harder than she would have expected.

"Who's behind everything?" she asked just to clarify.

He nodded.

She paused for a minute, stopping where she was on the trail as though that would help her figure out who in her little haven might want her dead.

Adam had no idea what he'd said to put that pained look on Shiloh's face, but he wished he could take it back and return her expression to the carefree one he'd seen on the boat earlier.

Of course, it was hours too late for that. Her entire de-meanor had changed when they'd set foot on this island. And he couldn't blame her. It was as if he could feel his-tory breathing down his neck here. And since most of the history with Blackbeard Island, from what he'd researched, either had to do with pirates or quarantines…well, neither evoked happy feelings.

But why the shaded look in her eyes now? The hardening of her features? Was it because he'd asked whom she suspected? It had been a straightforward-enough question, and with her analytical brain, he had a hard time believing it wasn't something she'd already thought through in detail.

But since she'd just come to an abrupt halt in front of him, nearly causing him to trip over her, it had apparently touched a nerve somewhere.

"Should we sit?" he asked, not waiting for an answer before he led her to the side of the trail and a log that would make a good bench. If her faraway look was an indication, she'd miss any clues she was searching for anyway if they kept walking, and he wasn't sure he was much help in that department. He was doing the best he could, but Shiloh was the cop. And a good one, too, he knew, despite how much he wished she could have chosen another career. Or just stuck with the first one.

She'd seemed happy with her job back then—and happy with him. But while the history professor she had been had seemed perfect for the businessman Adam once was, there was too much dividing the pastor and the policewoman.

He settled down beside her on the log. "Want to tell me what's got you so upset?"

She sat with her elbows on her knees, head between her hands. "Someone's trying to kill me."

He wasn't entirely sure how to reply to that.

Thankfully, she clarified, right after she let out a groan that just about broke his heart in two. "I've known that, obviously. But I hadn't really considered until recently that it's probably someone I know. But it makes sense. Either this guy is really, really good not to have drawn anyone's attention or he's a local." She choked out the last few words.

"I love that silly little town and the people. To think that one of them might…"

He heard her swallow hard and then she quit talking. Probably to keep from crying—he knew she couldn't stand that. She'd already come pretty close too many times lately for her taste.

He waited for a minute and sat quietly, listening to the bugs and frogs and whatever else was in these woods.

And then she drew a deep breath and spoke with a level of confidence that either scared him or made him proud— he had no idea how someone could shut off their emotions like that and wasn't sure it was a good thing, although it made her good at what she did.

"People it could be. Um, I suppose someone from the department could be involved." She lowered her voice. "Lieutenant Davies showed up at the scene of the shooting fast. Really fast. And running was something I decided to do right when I was leaving the chief's office. I told him I was going and left—someone must have overheard me to know that's where I'd be."

She paused. "Any of the EMTs who responded to the shooting could have been in the area because they were involved." She paused again. "Some random person in town is possible…even though I haven't even really talked to anyone else in the last few weeks—and Mary Hamilton, but I think we can be sure she's not involved. It's got to be someone who knows the area, though. Maybe I should look into who's running charter services to Blackbeard Island these days. Different people have done it over the years. That might be somewhere to start."

Adam nodded. Not much of a list, but he couldn't blame her. Now that he thought about it, it had to be a tough list to make.

"I'm ready again. Let's go." She stood up, and they resumed their trek down the trail.

Within minutes the scenery changed again—which it did a lot on this island—and the trail circled around a pond.

"Think it could be in that somewhere?" he asked, pointing at the murky water.

Shiloh shook her head. "Rumors about Blackbeard say he came and went from here a lot. If he wanted to be able to easily reach his stash then it would need to be somewhere relatively accessible. That's why I haven't bothered to venture off of the main trails. Well, that and snakes. But these paths are here because they were natural game trails, which means they're the ones animals, like deer, on this island would have been traveling even in Blackbeard's time. Wherever it is, it will be well hidden but easy to get to."

Her theory sounded logical enough but didn't put them any closer to finding the treasure. Adam picked up the pace to work out some of his frustration, since he didn't have a punching bag handy. The treasure was beginning to look impossible to find, the case harder and harder to solve.

TWELVE

Shiloh's breath caught in her throat, and chills crept down her arms and legs. The so-called bone graveyard, a vast span of dead trees on the north shore of Blackbeard Island, was like nothing she'd seen before.

The skeletons of trees stood there in the sand as if time had frozen them.

"What makes them do that?" she wondered softly, more to herself than anybody else.

"The ocean's taking over this spot of the island again. I read about it when I was researching. The tide has started to come all the way up here, and the consistent exposure to salt water kills the trees."

"And leaves their bones." Shiloh walked closer to the otherworldly area to inspect it. She'd been startled when Adam had first spoken up to answer her question. This was yet another place on the island where she felt as if she'd stepped into another world, away from everything that was familiar.

She stepped around one of the tree skeletons and walked away from the standing water, toward the shore. No sign of treasure that she could see.

What if there was no treasure at all in connection with Annie's death? But, no, there had to be. Shiloh had no reason to doubt it. The entire treasure probably wasn't gold—pirates like Blackbeard tended to diversify and much of the bounty would be parts of ships that were expensive and easy to sell—but there were too many reports of treasure for it to all just be a myth.

Still…what if the men had already found it? Maybe it was gone, and they had stuck around this part of Georgia only to make her pay for having the audacity to live when she should have died right along with her cousin.

The cracking of a tree branch in the forest just yards from the beach snapped Shiloh to attention. "Did you hear that?"

Adam had tensed, too; she could see it in the way he stood. "It's probably just an animal."

But she could tell the words were only meant to reassure her.

Shiloh shivered. "Let's get out of here."

"Aren't there still miles of beach left to cover?" He looked into her eyes as if searching for something.

Shiloh darted her gaze to the woods where she'd heard the sound, where she somehow felt as though someone was watching them. "Some other day, maybe. For now, we should go."

"Okay." He nodded slowly. "Which way?"

Shiloh pulled the map out of her pocket. "I think it's about an equal distance either way we go."

"Let's go the way we haven't been yet, then."

The glimmer in his eyes said he hadn't given up on finding a lead today. Shiloh hated the feeling of defeat she'd allowed to steal over her, but she was afraid she was being more realistic than Adam.

Just another reason a cop and a pastor were incompatible. It was her job to see the world the way it was—grit and sin and all. It was his job to see the best in people.

But the irrational feelings of warmth that stole over her as he grabbed her hand and walked on the beach alongside her defied logic. Maybe that was how falling in love was supposed to be.

Love…had she let herself admit yet that love might be exactly what she felt for Adam?

The walk seemed to take less time now that they were holding hands. She still kept her eyes open for any signs of criminal activity but she was certain the treasure wasn't here.

So where was it? Found—as she feared? Or hidden somewhere she hadn't yet suspected?

She and Adam stopped several times to rest and drink more water, ever since the hot Georgia sun had started beating down on them hours ago.

"We forgot to eat lunch," Shiloh remarked as she drained her last water bottle. She eyed the peanut-butter-and-jelly sandwiches she'd made last night. "Want one?"

Adam shook his head. "Too hot to eat."

He had a point. Besides, the sandwiches hadn't taken the heat well, either, and had mushed together in a less-than-appetizing way. Yeah, she'd skip lunch, also.

Finally, the boat dock was in sight.

"So is it just me—" she puffed between breaths "—or was this a more intense hike than you'd thought?"

Shiloh looked over at him and tried not to be jealous. The man was barely out of breath. She knew he worked out, but apparently he was in better shape than she'd realized.

He shrugged. "Yeah, it was tougher."

But nothing about him backed that up. In fact, she had a sneaking suspicion the only reason he'd said so was to make her feel better. Which was ridiculous. And very sweet.

They climbed into the boat, and Shiloh untied it and then navigated it down the creek back into open water.

"Take the wheel for a minute?" she asked Adam once they were cruising comfortably. He did so without hesitation, and she pulled her key chain from her pocket and unlocked the storage compartment. She reached for one of the water bottles, twisted open the cap and took a long drink, then reached for another to offer to Adam.

"Want one?" She reached it out toward him as she stood.

But the boat shifted under her as she did. Or maybe it was the sky above her that was moving. It tilted one way, then the other, and then everything swirled into chaos.

Right before it all went black.

One minute Shiloh had been standing, looking like her normal self and ready to resume her place as captain of her boat.

Seconds later she was sprawled on the deck, her skin a shade of greenish-gray that made Adam feel sick to his stomach.

He could see the mainland in the distance, but for now they were still in open water. He glanced at the horizon, then at Shiloh's prone form, debating his options and finally letting go of the wheel to get on his knees to check on her.

He wasn't a doctor, but her pulse seemed a little weaker to him than it should have been, and her forehead was warm. Of course, the warmth could be easily explained away by all their exercise and the sun bearing down on them. As for her loss of consciousness…dehydration was a possibility.

He eyed the water bottle on the floor next to her. Given her appearance, poison was an even better one.

He shook her gently. "Come on, Shiloh." No response. He hadn't expected one, but it had been worth a try. Realizing he was worthless as a doctor, he decided the best thing he could do was get them back to Treasure Point as fast as possible. It would be even better if he could divert their course and get to a bigger city that would have better poison-treatment options, but he would be lucky enough to remember the way back to where they'd come from.

The vibrations of the steering wheel beneath his hands as he increased his speed did a little to comfort him. At least he was doing what he could. He kept his eyes focused on shore and prayed harder than he ever had before.

The marsh that lined Treasure Point's shore grew closer, and he thought he could make out the channel he was supposed to take to get the boat back to the launch.

And then the boat sputtered. And began to cough in protest. He felt it shudder beneath him and glanced down to note that even the discordant motions weren't rousing Shiloh at all. He couldn't remember for sure from his first-aid classes from years ago, but he thought the longer someone was unconscious, the worse that was for them.

He was still staring at Shiloh, wondering why she wouldn't wake up, wondering what he was supposed to do about this malfunctioning boat, when it stopped right there in the water, maybe two hundred yards from shore. Waves tossed the boat, the sound of the spray seeming louder than it should. There were no other boats out. No people in sight.

They were alone. He looked back at Shiloh. Alone and likely running out of time.

Adam felt useless. He'd give anything to have the skills of a doctor or a mechanic. But he had neither. So he checked the only thing on the boat he really knew to check. The gas gauge.

Empty.

Hadn't Shiloh told him she'd checked the gas level twice? Either she'd missed something she should have seen…

He looked down at the half-empty water bottle beside Shiloh.

Or someone had poisoned her and then siphoned enough gas from the boat to get them tantalizingly close to help—but far enough away that they'd never make it in time.

Rage made his face heat, and he could hear his heart pounding in his ears. What kind of people did this? And how were he and Shiloh supposed to stop them when the bad guys were always one step ahead?

Dear Lord, please help us.

He bent down and felt Shiloh's pulse and forehead again. Her pulse remained the same, which he breathed a prayer of thanks for, but her forehead was burning hot.

Whatever drugs were in her system, they were working fast. And he was stuck here with no way of getting help.

He eyed the marshy shoreline. He could swim the distance easily enough, even fully dressed. But leaving Shiloh alone and unconscious when someone was making a habit of trying to kill her didn't seem like a good idea.

He realized with a pang that it was his fault she was lying there. She'd had all the water in her backpack, and he'd been the one to insist she take some out and leave them in the boat. Had someone overheard their conversation? Or just looked around her boat for something to sabotage and gotten lucky? He knew he'd locked that storage compartment, but picking the lock would be easy enough.

After several minutes of sitting, the boat getting tossed by the waves, he finally remembered his cell phone. He may not be able to physically do anything to help at the moment, but he could call for help.

One of the men at his church was a doctor. Adam found his number, which was programmed into his phone, and called him first. He explained the situation as fast as he could and agreed to meet the man at the launch ramp.

"Do you need me to call someone else for help?" Dr. Barry asked before he hung up.

"No, my next call is to the police chief. He'll be the fastest at getting someone out here." Or he could at least get hold of the Coast Guard or someone who could.

As Adam had suspected, the chief told him to look for someone within ten minutes. The heaviness in his stomach eased a little. Ten minutes. Just ten minutes until help arrived.

Then he looked at Shiloh's still body on the floor of the boat, the hair around her forehead getting damp with sweat from the fever she was running.

And he hoped ten minutes wouldn't be too late.

When what seemed like eternity had passed, Shiloh's eyes blinked open and Adam started to breathe again.

"Where are we?"

Her speech was a little muddled, but he supposed that was to be expected. Once Adam had gotten her to the doctor, described her symptoms and waited while the doctor had examined her, Adam had learned she'd been given dangerous levels of a common sedative—enough to kill her. The doctor had said if Adam had been thirty minutes later, she wouldn't have made it. The doctor had given her low doses of drugs to counteract the ones she'd been given and had pumped her full of fluid through an IV.

What followed were several agonizing hours of observation at the doctor's office. Once her vitals had shown signs of improvement and the doctor had declared she was in stable condition, they'd moved Shiloh to her house, where she'd be more comfortable. Adam and the doctor had settled a still-sleeping Shiloh onto her couch. Dr. Barry left to see other patients, instructing Adam to call if necessary but reassuring him that she'd be fine.

Relief had flooded Adam when the doctor had said that.

And then panic followed closely behind as he realized that whoever had tried to kill her once would likely try again.

"Adam?" Her tone said she'd called his name more than once, and he hadn't heard. He forced himself to stop dwelling on what could have happened and instead focus on the blessing that she was sitting in front of him, relatively unharmed.

"Are we at my house?" The frown on her face deepened. "My head is killing me."

He cringed at those words, knowing how close they'd been to coming true just hours before. "Yes, we're at your house."

"I remember being at the island." She squinted her eyes as if she was straining to see the memories materialize in front of her. "And I remember getting back to the boat. And being thirsty…"

"You were poisoned." His voice was flat. Matter-of-fact. He wished he could soften it into something more reassuring for Shiloh's sake, but was there any nice way to cushion those words anyway?

"I feel like death."

He really wished she'd quit using words like *killing* and *death.* Did the woman not realize she held his heart firmly in her hands and that this went beyond wanting her to be safe, that he actually *needed* her to be safe?

In that instant he saw he was in a lose-lose situation. He could side with the chief, who had been none too happy to learn they'd been at Blackbeard Island and clearly suspected it had something to do with the case. If Adam took that route, he'd tell her that she needed to give up the case and let the other officers handle it. She looked vulnerable enough right now that she might listen.

But then he'd be doing the same thing he had done before—not supporting her after Annie's death when she'd told him that she wanted to become a police officer. Maybe not now, but eventually she'd resent him for that.

Or he could let her keep working and maybe have her end up…hurt worse than she was today.

Either way, it was looking as if he was going to lose her. And Adam wasn't happy just to sit by and let that happen. He might not be the best partner for solving a puzzle as complex as this one was turning out to be, but he was strong and muscular enough to work as a bodyguard. He knew without a doubt that he wasn't leaving her property until the chief listened to reason and put a guard near her house.

This had gone beyond professional—whoever was after Shiloh was getting too personal. She and Adam hadn't even uncovered anything lately, which made the escalation in the threat against her even more unreasonable.

Or had they discovered more than they thought? Enough that the criminals watching them were getting scared?

He turned his attention back to Shiloh. "I'm sorry you feel so bad. It's all the drugs in your system—the bad ones and the ones that are working against those."

She nodded, closing her eyes again. "I'm so tired, but I can't go back to sleep."

He couldn't blame her. After today, he wasn't sure he'd ever sleep again.

"Talk to me about something."

He hated how bad she must be feeling but loved hearing her voice ask him for help, knowing he could make her feel better. "About what?"

She shrugged. "Anything. Maybe about your house and how you want it to look, so I can figure out how we're going to decorate it."

"'We'?"

She blushed. "Not 'we'…like that. Just thought I'd help you get it set up. It's too *typical bachelor* right now. You have a living room and basically nothing else. I saw your room when I walked by it on the way to the bathroom. You are in desperate need of some furniture."

He'd already realized it needed a woman's touch. "In my defense, my library is set up, too."

"You have a library?" Her eyes fluttered open, and he could see he'd sparked her interest.

"Sure. I love to read. You know that. I've got quite the book collection, actually."

"On shelves, even? Not just stacked on the floor?"

Her voice was still slurred, but the return of her sense of humor and ability to tease him reassured him that her condition was improving.

"On shelves. You should come look sometime. I can't believe I didn't tell you to when you were over the other day. Especially with how much you love staring at books." He laughed when he thought about their time at the widow's house. "Did you memorize everything in Mary Hamilton's library the day we were there? You'd come in handy as a kind of modern card-catalog system."

"Ha-ha."

She tried to glare, but with the sleepiness in her gaze, it lost some fierceness in the translation and just ended up looking cute.

"I was trying to remember all the books she has. You never know—some little detail like that could tie in to the case."

"So you say."

A couple of seconds went by, and Adam searched his mind for another topic, but a glance down at Shiloh told him that she'd finally fallen back asleep. He reached for the light blanket on the back of her couch and covered her with it, then returned to his chair. It was already past ten o'clock at night, and his stomach was protesting the fact that he hadn't eaten since breakfast, but he had no intention of leaving Shiloh's side anytime soon.

In fact, when he did leave her two hours later, realizing that as long as they weren't married he couldn't stay in her house alone with her all night long, he only went as far as the driveway. Adam felt a little relief when he saw a patrol car parked across the street from her house, a couple of doors down. The chief must have sent someone to keep an eye on the place.

It made him feel better, but still—he wanted to know for himself that she was okay. Adam unlocked his car, leaned the seat back, set his cell phone on the armrest and closed his eyes. At least this way he'd be close enough to come immediately if she called. No one was getting to Shiloh. Not tonight. Not if he could help it.

THIRTEEN

Morning came, bringing along with it the closest thing to a hangover Shiloh had ever experienced. Her head throbbed, and she felt a little as if she'd been run over by a lawn mower. Not to mention she had some kind of pain in her back.

She shifted to get more comfortable, noting finally that she wasn't in her bed but on her couch.

Yesterday came rushing back to her with all the grace of an entire team of football players.

At least that explained the headache. The pain in her back was probably from sleeping on the couch. And the run-over feeling was likely a side effect of someone almost succeeding in taking her out of the picture.

Details from the day before were fuzzy, but she did remember Adam sitting with her. In fact, she remembered starting to wake up several times early in the evening, panic overtaking her from the nightmares that had invaded her sleep, but he had been there and each time had made gentle *shushing* noises and had held her hand until she'd fallen back asleep.

She looked around the room. He wasn't here now. Of course not. It wouldn't look right if he'd stayed all night.

Dragging the blanket she was covered in with her, Shiloh shuffled to her bedroom, determined to go back to sleep.

A knock at the door made other thoughts enter her mind. Was it Adam? Or someone coming to finish the job he'd botched yet again? Of course, criminals didn't usually knock…but maybe it was a ruse to get her outside?

Shiloh rubbed her head. She definitely needed more sleep to recover. Either way, she wasn't answering that door. She climbed into bed, taking her cell phone out of her pocket and setting it on her bedside table.

The knock on the door grew more frantic. Shiloh pulled up the covers over her.

Then her cell phone rang, the shrillness of the ringtone making her wince. "Hello?" Her voice didn't sound so great. All in all, yesterday had not been the best day of her life.

"Shiloh, are you okay?"

Adam's voice carried a panicked urgency—she was coherent enough for that to register. She tried to summon her senses to full alert but still felt groggy around the edges—a normal, though frustrating, side effect. "What's wrong?" she shot back.

"With me? Nothing. What about you?" Now he seemed confused. Which confused her. Why wouldn't she be okay?

"I'm fine. I mean, considering."

"Then why didn't you answer your door?"

"That was you?"

"Yeah. I finally woke up and wanted to check on you."

"So you drove all the way over here? Don't you have to work at some point? I don't want to cause your job to suffer." And to her surprise, it was true. The more she had watched Adam, the more she'd seen him live out his Christianity in little ways, like being so kind to the widow. His dad hadn't been like that—he'd been more into the power of leadership, Shiloh had always thought, than in truly following Christ.

Not so with Adam. In fact, the way he lived was enough to tempt her to darken the door of a church again, something she hadn't done since shortly after her cousin had been killed.

Sunday, she thought resolutely. She'd go Sunday and surprise him.

"...didn't need to drive because I stayed here."

Adam was explaining something. She'd missed the first part, but his point was clear enough. He'd been here? All night? "You weren't inside. At least, I didn't see you."

"Nah. I've been out in your driveway."

She peeked out of the window and saw his vehicle, as well as a police cruiser across the street. Shiloh smiled.

Adam must have slept in the car. That meant he'd probably slept far less comfortably than even Shiloh had on the couch. Something warmed inside her to know he hadn't wanted to leave her. It made her feel...safe.

"You're the sweetest man I've ever known—do you know that?"

"Just trying to make sure you're safe."

Now that she knew he hadn't slept well, she could hear the deep gruffness in his voice that betrayed how tired he was.

"Why don't you head home and get some sleep?"

"Someone should stay here and watch your house."

"I'm guessing that's what the car across the street is for." She smiled a little as she said it. "I appreciate that you stayed last night. But really, one bodyguard will be okay for a little while."

He was considering her request. So as long as he was being reasonable, she made another.

"So go home and work on your sermon some more or

something. I've kept you away from your office enough this week, and I don't want a half-done sermon my first time in church in years."

It took a second for her statement to register with him. "You're coming?" Pleasure and surprise fought for dominance in his tone.

Both made her smile. Even though returning to church was for her, something she wanted to do, it was nice to be able to do something to make him happy. "I thought I would, yeah."

"Great—that's awesome. You have no idea how happy that makes me, Shiloh."

Anticipation churned in Shiloh's stomach. She was nervous about going back to church for the first time in years. But she was ready, and it was something she needed to do. Partially because she wanted a future with Adam and knew that would entail being more involved in church.

But mostly because she could see God working in her life again, not only in keeping her alive through so many attacks, but also in giving her peace at times when her circumstances were the opposite of peaceful, and she was willing—hesitant, but willing—to take steps toward trusting Him again. She still saw no logic behind Him allowing her cousin to be killed, but He'd kept Shiloh alive so many times now that she couldn't deny His care and involvement.

"Okay," Adam finally conceded. "If you're sure you'll be fine, I'll go catch a few more hours of sleep and then go work at the office. On the condition that we have dinner together tonight."

The prospect of seeing him brightened her outlook on the day. She'd gotten so used to his presence, with them riding together at work, that spending an extended period of the day without him felt as if something was missing. "Sounds good to me. I can cook something, I'm sure."

"No. I'll bring takeout. Pizza or Chinese?"

"Chinese sounds delicious, but you won't find any in Treasure Point." One of the few downsides to life in a small town.

"You leave the details to me. If it's Chinese you want, it's Chinese you'll have."

She laughed at the chivalry in his tone over something so inconsequential. But it was nice to be taken care of. She could definitely get used to this.

"I'll look forward to it."

"See you tonight, then."

Shiloh shut her phone and settled back into her bed. Her whole body still felt the aftereffects of the day before, but her mind was racing to find new possibilities. She refused to let yesterday's defeat paralyze her. She might not be able to get out and investigate, but she had contacts she could get in touch with and talk to about history and pirate lore. Maybe something in one of those conversations could give her another lead.

She picked up her phone and dialed Professor Slate, her former mentor and the head of the history department at the college where she used to work.

"Professor Slate here."

"Good morning, it's Shiloh Evans. How are you?"

"Shiloh, how are you?"

She fought the urge to laugh at the reply she *could* give but gave a safe answer. "I'm fine."

"Still taking time off from teaching?"

They'd emailed a few times since she had left, and while Professor Slate had seemed to understand her desire to take a break from teaching, he'd told her many times that he had hoped she'd return someday. She hadn't told him what she was doing instead—he had probably assumed she was researching, learning more about history. Which was basically true at the moment.

"Yes, I'm enjoying it. I can't step away from the subject of history completely, though. It seems like there are always questions I need to find answers to."

Professor Slate's low laugh filled her ears. "I can relate to that. Let me know if I can help in any way. I know I've benefited before from getting a colleague and fellow history lover's opinion."

Shiloh saw her opening and took it. "Actually, I would love your thoughts on Blackbeard. You know how much interest I've always taken in studying Georgia's pirate history."

"Thinking about making it the subject of your thesis and going for a doctorate? You should, Shiloh. It would be very beneficial professionally. You know if you ever want to teach here again, I'll make sure there's a spot for you, but that would be easier with a more advanced degree."

"I appreciate that," she told him sincerely, dancing around his question.

"As far as Blackbeard, we know he spent time near Savannah. People have even found small stashes of coins that are rumored to have been his. He's said to have left larger stashes of treasures farther south, I believe, between Savannah and Florida." He switched to his professor voice. "It would have been impossible for pirates to use a bank, so they'd have to store their treasures in places where they could access them, make withdrawals and deposits as needed." He sighed. "But you probably know all of that. I don't know many additional specifics. I'm sorry I can't help you more."

"I appreciate what you've been able to tell me, though. Isn't it interesting how history and economics tie so closely together?"

"It is. That sounds like a subject to explore in a doctoral thesis."

Shiloh smiled. "It does, doesn't it? Thanks again and have a good day, sir."

She hung up and shook her head. Back to square one. But at least she was left with this reassurance—if someone as well educated as Professor Slate didn't have any better guess for the location of Blackbeard's famous treasure than "between Savannah and Florida," then chances were that the criminals hadn't found it yet, either. Which meant she still had a chance to be the first to reach it.

It was amazing what a few hours of sleep in a comfortable bed could do. Adam had come home and crashed. He'd woken rested and refreshed and ready to head to the office. He'd found a message on his voice mail after he'd gotten out of the shower from someone at the church who had nice things to say about his recent sermon and had also wanted to set up a counseling appointment sometime in the next week.

It had been less than two weeks, but it seemed as though he'd been trying to prove himself to the people of Treasure Point for a lifetime, and finally, they were letting him in. No longer did he have occasional doubts whispering in his ear about whether or not he was the man for this job. He still knew he couldn't do any of it without God—Adam hadn't gotten that dumb or prideful—but finally, he felt as if he was accomplishing something for God's Kingdom.

He was humming as he walked across the church parking lot. When he reached the building, he noticed the door was already unlocked. He felt his shoulders tense. Maybe he'd left them unlocked the last time he'd been here. Or maybe one of the groups who met here had. Surely danger from the treasure hunters wouldn't follow him into a church building.

He breathed a sigh of relief when he discovered it hadn't.

And then caught his breath again as he realized danger in another form had found him—all of the board members were sitting or standing in his office. Waiting. And with them was a very disgruntled older woman who he'd been warned was a gossip.

None of this looked good.

Still, he'd done nothing wrong and responses to his sermons had been good, so he forced a smile. "Good afternoon, gentlemen, Mrs. Winslow. I didn't see your cars outside. How can I help you?"

"We walked over, actually," one of them clarified.

This was feeling more and more like an ambush. He reached his hand to his throat to loosen his tie and then realized he didn't have a tie on—it was just the almost-palpable tension in the room causing his throat to tighten.

"How can I help you?" he repeated.

"We have a moral issue to discuss with you, Pastor." One of the men spoke up, his voice more serious than Adam had ever heard it.

Adam eyed Mrs. Winslow, wondering what her part in this was and if the board intended to have this whole unofficial meeting in front of her. Generally, church matters were handled confidentially. Unless Mrs. Winslow herself had the moral issue. And from the sour look on her face, as though she was eager to see someone pay for whatever horrendous crime she thought they'd committed, he doubted it was her issue personally.

"All right, well, let's discuss it. Should we go somewhere with more room?"

"We're fine here."

Adam sat in his chair. He was slightly uncomfortable sitting since so many of the men were standing, but it was clearly what they wanted him to do.

"Look, Pastor, let's shoot straight here. We've heard some

upsetting news about you being at a woman's house all night." Hal Smith, one of the more down-to-earth members of the congregation, spoke up. Adam felt himself relax. His presence at Shiloh's, sleeping in her driveway, was easily explainable and within the bounds of what he'd consider moral.

Maybe there was a way to defuse this situation after all.

"I assume you're referring to last night?"

He was answered by grim nods.

"Shiloh Evans was almost killed yesterday." He hesitated to give too many details for fear it could jeopardize the case somehow, but news in a small town traveled fast. He was surprised they hadn't already heard, especially since the doctor was a member of this congregation.

"I was with her when she was poisoned, and after she received treatment, I stayed with her inside until she'd passed through the worst of the ill effects. Once I felt okay about leaving her, I went outside and slept in my car. I didn't feel comfortable with her not having someone close she could call in case there was more trouble." He eyed the stack of commentaries on his desk, his mind already shifting to focus on Sunday's sermon. "Was there anything else I could clarify for you?"

A moment of pregnant silence passed. Adam felt his tension returning. Shouldn't this be the point where they laughed off the misunderstanding and went about their business?

"See, but there's still the appearance of evil there, Pastor."

He was hardly paying attention to who was doing the talking anymore, since all of their voices seemed joined against him in some kind of lynch-mob mentality.

"'The appearance of evil'?" He felt his blood pressure rise. "I'm well aware of the necessity of avoiding that. But in certain circumstances I think being practical is more important. Anyone——" he turned his gaze on Mrs. Winslow, since it appeared she was most likely the *informant* here "——who saw my car parked in front of Shiloh's house could have walked over to it and seen that I was sleeping in it. Alone. And was not in her house past a little after midnight."

"That's still awfully late."

What part about her being poisoned did these people not understand? And what was it he was on trial for here, anyway? "I wasn't aware there was a certain hour past which I wasn't allowed to be inside someone's house." He heard the attitude in his words, knew it probably wasn't his best move, but felt powerless to change his tone. He silently prayed for help and took several deep breaths.

"It's not just that. We believe you that nothing inappropriate happened."

He relaxed slightly.

"At the same time, we know this isn't the first time you've been at her house late. And we think it's important, for your ministry, that you're more careful about how things look."

In normal circumstances, he could see they were right. Last night was still an exception in his mind, but maybe in everyday circumstances he should make sure to be out of her house early enough that neighboring busybodies didn't have anything to get themselves all in a tizzy about.

"And it's Shiloh Evans herself, Pastor."

"Shiloh… I'm not sure what you mean."

The men shifted uncomfortably.

Good. He wanted them to.

"If you're going to get caught carrying on with someone…"

He thought they had established there was no *carrying on.*

"It should at least be someone…suitable. A pastor has to marry a certain kind of woman, you know…" Hal had the good grace to blush. "She's not really *pastor's wife* material."

"She hasn't even been to church since she moved to town," someone mumbled.

"It's not that we think it's our right to choose who you date," another chimed in. "But if you're not careful, you'll make decisions that could affect your ministry here, drive people away from the church. We know it's going above and beyond to concern ourselves in your personal…friendships, but don't you think someone's spiritual life, maybe even their salvation, is more important than who you'd prefer to date?"

"Wait—am I hearing this right?" Adam interrupted. "You're not upset that the car in her driveway looked bad, which I've already explained. You're upset that I've been spending time with Shiloh specifically? She loves this town, the people here. And I was under the impression everyone liked her, too."

"We do. Everyone loves Shiloh—as a person—and respects her. But you're a pastor. The woman you date should be someone who is already involved in the church, who *goes* to church. Not just a well-respected member of the community."

Adam's head pounded, and he caught a glimpse of how Shiloh must've felt after waking up with that poison in her system. Even though it was technically Shiloh they objected to, it seemed almost like a personal affront—that they didn't trust him to make these decisions for himself and to be a good judge of character.

He wanted to fight back somehow. At the same time…

he knew they were right about Shiloh not attending church. Not that church attendance was the sole basis for a relationship with God, but it did say something. Or did it? Didn't he know Shiloh, know that her heart was in the right place? But did he have the right to put his opinions and beliefs ahead of those of his congregation? If his choices made them uncomfortable, and harmed their trust in him, wasn't that reason enough for him to reconsider?

He was called to this job. He knew he was. And though he cared deeply for Shiloh, he couldn't sacrifice God's call to have the relationship with her that he'd wanted for years…could he?

Adam rubbed his temples.

"I think we've given you enough to think about. You'll make the right decision."

The men and Mrs. Winslow filed out silently. Adam didn't look up from where he sat staring at his desk, but he heard the last man pull the door shut behind him.

They'd gone about this wrong. Adam knew that much. But their hearts appeared to be genuinely in the right place. And he couldn't deny their accusations. Though he knew Shiloh was a Christian, she hadn't spent much time in church in years. Was that a bad witness for him to date someone who didn't outwardly prioritize faith in her life? Was he putting his own desires ahead of what God wanted and what was best for the congregation where Adam believed God had sent him?

He looked up and whispered a prayer, but no audible voice spoke from beyond the ceiling, telling him what to do. In his heart he believed the deacons' accusations were unfair. But when he thought about it logically, and about the progress he'd made in the past two weeks, such as the people who had opened up to him, he knew he didn't want to sacrifice that.

"Is this what You want, God?" he asked aloud, hoping somehow that speaking the words would make God's answer clearer.

But he got nothing. All he could sense was his own desire to succeed in this job. Make God proud. Make his dad proud.

While the thought of backing off from this relationship with Shiloh, even a little, felt as if someone was ripping out Adam's heart and stomping on it, he couldn't give up on his calling so easily.

He couldn't fail at this. With sickening clarity, he realized he'd been left with no choice.

FOURTEEN

The clock had just chimed six when the doorbell rang. Shiloh's stomach growled, and she laughed at her hunger as she walked to open the door.

"Hi!" she greeted with a smile.

Only it wasn't Adam. It was Matt O'Dell. He held a bag of take-out Mexican food in front of him. "Adam sent this. He dropped it off a few minutes ago and asked if I could bring it to you. I'm supposed to tell you he can't make it tonight. But he's sorry." O'Dell raised an eyebrow. "What is this, middle school and I'm the messenger?"

Shiloh's heart dropped to her stomach, which was ridiculous, since there wasn't really anything going on with Adam anyway. Or there shouldn't be. She shrugged. "Sorry you got caught in the middle. Thanks for passing on the message." She motioned to the car outside. "And for keeping watch out there."

His face sobered. "I'm glad to do that. I don't like that someone's after you, Shiloh."

"Well, I appreciate it." She smiled at him, thankful he was the guy watching her house. She liked Matt. Maybe even would have considered him attractive if she hadn't still been in love with Adam when they'd first met after she'd come to town. Now he was more like a brother.

She took the bag from him and motioned inside. "Want to come in and eat? It looks like there's plenty."

"Nah." He was already shaking his head. "I need to stay out here where I can see the perimeter. But thanks. Have a good night, Shiloh."

And then he was gone, and she was alone again. Shiloh reached into her pocket to see if she'd missed a call from Adam on her cell only to realize she'd left it on the kitchen counter. She picked it up and checked the screen. No missed calls. No new messages.

The exhaustion she'd been fighting since she'd gotten up from her nap threatened to overwhelm her again but the hunger gnawing at her stomach won out. Shiloh opened one of the to-go boxes and took a few bites of the house special, then decided she wasn't hungry after all.

She put the food in the fridge.

Then she checked the door locks, turned out the lights and went to sleep.

The first thing Shiloh did when she woke up the next morning was to check for messages from Adam. There weren't any.

So she did what any self-respecting woman would do. She drove to town to the coffee shop and ordered herself a large latte with extra whip.

Surely he hadn't lost interest in her all within a matter of hours, she reasoned with herself as she walked from the coffee shop back to her car.

Still, she felt odd about the fact that she hadn't heard from him. But she refused to put her life or investigation on hold because of her feelings.

She unlocked her car and climbed in, driving straight in the direction of Mary Hamilton's house. As Shiloh had showered this morning, it had occurred to her that the treasure could be hidden farther inland. The town had gotten its name from rumors of pirate treasure, but Shiloh had never taken those rumors seriously. Maybe there was something to them after all. And if anyone would know, Mary Hamilton would.

Besides, she reasoned as she took another sip of her latte and navigated her way down the long driveway to Mary's house, if a pirate was going to hide his treasure in town, the Hamilton estate was as logical a location as any. Shiloh laughed out loud. She was probably reaching with that one; she'd seen the house for herself and knew it wasn't nearly old enough to have been standing when Blackbeard had haunted these shores. But the residence did come awfully close to the water...

She took a long look around as she pulled her car in, enjoying the old Southern feeling of the estate and the beautiful weather. Nothing about the place was foreboding today. She parked her car and walked toward the long sidewalk that would take her to the house.

She'd almost reached the pathway when she saw the flash of an explosion, and an invisible wall of heat threw her backward and to the ground.

The boom registered just as she hit the dirt. She lay still, not sure if she should or could move, spitting dirt out of her mouth and trying to decide if any bones were broken.

Then urgency jolted her to action. Mary was still in that house. Shiloh had seen her car parked in the detached garage. Shiloh rolled to her side and sat up, turning to face the blast's point of origin.

The entire structure—every beautiful, carefully crafted, historical piece—was engulfed in angry orange flames.

She forced herself to stay on the ground, fighting against the urge to run inside to find Mary. A blast that inclusive most likely would have killed the old woman within seconds, and the flames were so widespread by this point that Shiloh knew she didn't have the training to get inside and come back out alive.

She fumbled in her pocket for her cell phone and dialed the fire department.

"There's a fire—an explosion—at the Hamilton estate," she told the dispatcher. "This is Officer Shiloh Evans from the police department. I saw the whole thing, and I'm okay, but Widow Hamilton…" Shiloh choked back sobs as the horror of what she was watching enveloped her as the smoke did. "I believe she was inside."

"We have a truck on its way." The woman's professional tone never wavered. Shiloh knew the dispatchers were trained for that, but Shiloh didn't know how they actually did it. She couldn't keep herself detached any longer.

As she waited for the fire department to show up—along with the police department, who she was sure had been notified, given the suspicious circumstances—Shiloh tried desperately to focus her eyes on something besides the flames and the crumbling structure before her.

But she couldn't look away.

She had no idea how long it took for the emergency vehicles to arrive. Probably not long. But Shiloh had time to run through a thousand different scenarios. What if she'd come sooner? Would she have noticed something suspicious and been able to convince Mary to leave? Or would she just have found herself a victim of the blast, too?

Along with sadness and anger over Mary's death, thoughts about the probable killers vied for attention in her brain. Had her gut feeling that this place could somehow be linked to the treasure been correct? She tried to dismiss that thought, but why would the men have destroyed the entire building, killing a woman in the process, if that weren't the case?

Perhaps she'd never know. Shiloh hated it when life didn't

resolve itself the way she wanted it to and left her with un-answered questions.

She hated it most of all when her failure to find answers meant that someone else got hurt.

She was shivering, though it was at least eighty degrees even without the heat of the fire, which was making the sur-rounding area much hotter. She recognized it as a symptom of shock but did her best to ignore it as she finally stood and walked numbly to where the chief stood, watching the horrific scene unfold.

"The explosion appears to be intentional, from what they're seeing so far," he confided as she approached.

She had expected nothing less. Gut instinct had told her that and had also told her that the men who had done this were the ones who were after her. How had Mary got-ten involved?

Firefighters swarmed into the building, coming out one by one, empty-handed, shaking their heads.

If Mary had been inside, and Shiloh knew from the pres-ence of Mary's car that she must have been, they couldn't find her.

Shiloh turned from the chief and ran several feet away to lose her latte in the bushes by an old oak tree.

"This is getting out of hand," she heard the chief mut-ter to himself as she returned. She agreed wholeheartedly, though it was a gross understatement.

They stood in silence together, just watching. It seemed as though half the town had gathered already, held back to a safe distance by a few of the officers and rolls of police tape, to see what was happening. Shiloh could hear some of them crying and others making comments in voices that betrayed their unease that something like this could hap-pen in their town.

"We'll need to get a statement from you, since you saw it," the chief stated in a matter-of-fact way.

Shiloh nodded; she'd been expecting this.

"And, Shiloh?"

She looked up at him.

"I'm extending your leave indefinitely. You have until Tuesday to come clean with what you know about this case. Do it then or you're benched for the foreseeable future."

She felt the blow straight to her core. Five days, if she counted today. That was how long she had to solve a case that had been plaguing her for five years. Or she had to admit defeat. Start life over somewhere else.

And keep running from a past that wouldn't stay there.

Adam closed his sermon on Sunday with the knowledge that fewer than half of his congregation had heard a word he'd said. Most likely even less of them had been impacted.

The explosion at Mary Hamilton's house had rocked the town to the core, and his congregation had been no exception. He'd deviated from the sermon he'd already prepared and instead had preached something that might comfort and encourage them, with Scriptures about how the body of Christ should react in such circumstances.

And it had fallen on deaf ears.

He kept a smile pasted to his face as he shook hands and retreated to his office as soon as he could. Had Shiloh been there? He hadn't noticed, but he'd been less focused today than he could ever remember being.

In short, today's was the worst sermon he had ever preached.

He shut his office door a little too hard and sank into his desk chair. Wasn't he trying his best, doing everything he could to minister to these people? He'd even pulled back from his relationship with Shiloh to reevaluate it and make sure the board wasn't right. So why now, when his congregation so badly needed his guidance, had he been unable to find words to reach them? Was his own turmoil standing between him and the people he most wanted to help?

The uneasiness in his stomach every time he thought of Shiloh made him wonder if he'd made the right choice in that area.

The worst part of it—if there was a part worse than missing Shiloh's company every second of the day—was that he hadn't explained why he'd backed off. When he pictured the look on her face as he disappeared out of her life this time—not the other way around—it made him want to shake himself for treating her that way.

Adam closed his eyes and tried to pray, but just like after the deacons had met with him on Thursday, he couldn't get farther than the ceiling.

"God, what am I doing wrong?"

Everything within him hated the thought of failing this church. And not just because it was a ministry. Maybe a little pride was involved, as well. Still, he'd tried to give 100 percent of himself to this job. A hollow feeling inside Adam told him that, for the past several days, it wasn't working.

Maybe you're not enough.

The words jolted him. That was what God wanted him to know? That despite his best efforts, he was a failure after all?

A Scripture he'd learned early on in seminary found its way to the forefront of his mind. *I am the vine; you are the branches. The one who remains in Me and I in him produces much fruit, because you can do nothing without Me.* It was John 15:5, and Adam could remember distinctly the day during his Bible reading that this truth had jumped out at him. He'd written it on an index card to memorize.

So this was about him trying to please God in Adam's

own strength? Closer inspection of what he'd done told him that was true. He had felt nothing but peace from God when he'd decided to pursue Shiloh again and had felt confirmation that doing so was right. But when the board had implied that was the wrong decision, had Adam even asked God?

Or had he just decided it was what he needed to do in his own strength so he could reach these people?

His circumstances were suddenly clearer to him than they'd been in days. He was going about this the wrong way. He should be mindful of his congregation's needs—and become all things to all people, as Paul had said in the book of First Corinthians.

But he also needed to listen to God's leading and depend on God's strength and not things he could do himself.

Adam fought the urge to bang his head against his desk. Why was he so dumb sometimes?

He grabbed his car keys and reached for the office door, turning out the light as he went. He'd left Shiloh without a partner for too long already, and he wasn't going to leave her abandoned any longer.

FIFTEEN

By the time Shiloh's phone showed Adam's number on the caller-ID screen, she wasn't sure she wanted to talk to him anyway. She'd gone home, alone, from the widow's house that Friday, had eaten cereal for dinner and had cried herself to sleep, unable to banish the mental video of the explosion from her mind.

She answered anyway.

"I'm sorry, Shiloh."

She'd say this much for him: he'd chosen a good opening line. "Sorry?"

He sighed. "You know what for. I'm sorry for ditching you for dinner the other night. Sorry for not giving you an explanation, not being there when you heard about the widow."

"I didn't hear about her, Adam. I was there. Watched every second as her house exploded and burned to the ground."

Her tone tasted bitter as the words left her mouth. Like she'd done over and over for the past two days, she tried to blink the pictures from her mind.

If only it would work.

"I'm sorry." His voice broke, carrying a depth of emotion that gave the words even more impact. Shiloh relaxed her tensed shoulders, wanting more than anything to fix what was wrong between them and feel him wrap her in one of those everything-will-be-okay hugs again.

"Okay." She let out a breath she hadn't realized she'd been holding.

"Let me make things up to you. I've got that Chinese takeout I promised you in the seat beside me—I drove up to Savannah right after church to get it. Come over to my house, and we'll have a late lunch or an early dinner, whichever you want to call it, and I can tell you again how sorry I am."

Chinese food? She liked how he did apologies. Although she wasn't sure she was ready to forgive and forget quite yet. But she could at least hear him out. She checked her watch. "Won't you have to be back at church soon?"

"No, we've been having some plumbing issues and one of the lines burst during Sunday school. The plumber can't come until tomorrow and strongly advised canceling to-night."

"I'll see you soon, then." She paused, feeling uncertain all of a sudden. "When should I come?"

"I'll be there in about ten minutes. Come as soon as you can. I can't wait to see you."

Shiloh hung up the phone and looked at herself in the mirror. She had gone to church this morning, so her hair and makeup were okay, but she had already changed out of her Sunday dress. Her present outfit was the classic feel-sorry-for-herself variety—oversize sweats and a T-shirt.

She changed into one of her nicer pairs of jeans and a dark blue short-sleeved shirt that she'd been told brought out her eyes.

Not that she was trying to make Adam notice her eyes or anything.

Shiloh slipped on a pair of black flats, dropped her Glock

into her purse and headed out the door. She didn't normally carry her gun when she wasn't on duty, but with everything that had happened in the past few weeks, it would be smart to be prepared.

When she pulled up to Adam's house, his car was already in the driveway. She took a deep breath and walked to the front door. Before she could ring the bell, he opened the door and swept her into his arms for a hug.

"I've missed you so much," his deep voice said softly in her ear.

She pulled away, not willing to let her guard down completely after how much the past few days had hurt. "You could have seen me if you'd wanted to."

"I know, Shiloh. You have to believe when I say I'm sorry. Really sorry. I was wrong. Come in, please, and let me tell you how stupid I was."

She stepped inside and inhaled the tangy smell of Chinese takeout. "That smells amazing."

"I hope it tastes good, too. I wasn't sure where the best place was to get it, and you said there wasn't any in Treasure Point itself, so I just went to that place in Savannah we used to go to."

Shiloh grinned. "No wonder it smells so incredible."

"Please—" he motioned to where the boxes were lined up on the kitchen counter "—help yourself."

They both filled their plates, then sat down at the table. Once Adam had prayed and they'd started eating, Shiloh found herself growing nervous. As strange as he'd been acting the past couple of days, she didn't know what to expect.

Doubts and questions crowded into her mind until it distracted her from the Chinese food—which was clearly unacceptable.

"Adam, what's up?" she asked as she set her fork down.

"You said that you were sorry for…acting weird the last couple of days. And it's okay. But what's going on now?"

He exhaled and nodded, as if he'd seen her questions coming. "You have to promise not to say anything until I'm done explaining."

She raised her eyebrows. Not her favorite condition, but she could live with it. "Okay."

"It was stupid, Shiloh, really stupid. But some people managed to convince me that my dating you was going to hurt my ministry at the church. I didn't want that, so I pulled back."

He shrugged, as if this should all be easy to understand.

Meanwhile, she blinked back surprise. Hurt his ministry…? Sure, her church-attendance record had been nonexistent in Treasure Point, but that didn't make her less of a Christian. And she was mending that relationship with God now. "I don't think I understand what you mean."

Adam shook his head. "I told you, it's stupid. And now I see I should have known better. Basically, they were concerned about how late I've been at your house several times…"

Okay, there had been extenuating circumstances, but he was a pastor, and she could see how that might make some uncomfortable. But that was solved easily enough by a simple explanation and wouldn't have required any major changes to their relationship. "And…?"

He shifted uncomfortably in his chair. Aha. There had been more.

"You're not… They pointed out that you're not…the type of woman people expect a pastor to date."

"Because I work?" She raised her eyebrows. She'd known parts of this town were stuck in an old-fashioned mind-set, but with the economy the way it was, she'd have thought they'd be less resistant to something like that.

But Adam was shaking his head. "Not exactly. It's mostly your lack of church attendance. I admit I had some second thoughts because of your job."

The deacons having a problem with her infrequent visits to church she understood. But Adam being bothered by her being a cop? How many times were they going to break up or almost break up because of that issue?

She pushed her chair back from the table. "I should go."

He reached for her hand to stop her. "No, don't. I realized they're wrong. I know how important your faith is to you, even if you haven't been to church much lately. And I was wrong about your job."

This she had to hear. She edged her chair back toward the table.

"A pastor's wife carrying a gun and fighting crime is not exactly typical. But, Shiloh, if we ever decide to pursue our relationship to the point of marriage, it will be because I love you for who you are. And just like you being a history professor was a big part of you when I met you, being a cop is part of you now. My reason for struggling with it has nothing to do with not believing in you. It's just…" He shook his head. "See, the thing is, Shiloh, before my dad and I moved to Savannah, we lived in Florida."

She stilled. Adam had never wanted to talk about his childhood. Besides the fact that his mom hadn't been around for some of it, Shiloh knew nothing.

"My mom was in the Coast Guard. They were running drug interdictions, and she boarded a ship to perform a search and didn't make it off."

"Oh, Adam." She laid a hand on his arm, grief threatening to overwhelm her on his behalf.

"It's okay now. I mean, it still hurts. But I'm okay. She died doing something she loved, something she felt called to do. But it was dangerous work. And my dad had always resented it, did even more after she was killed. It's why…" He hesitated. "It's why I've been so against your job. But I was wrong to let my fears take over. Even when you were a history professor, you had spunk, Shiloh, like my mom. I think that's part of the reason I was attracted to you. The job you have now fits who you are."

He cleared his throat. "I don't want you to change, Shiloh. Besides, you're good at what you do. Our country needs more law-enforcement officers with talent like yours. And, yes, I wish you could step back and let someone else do it. And, yes, it scares me to think of marrying you and having children and worrying that one day their mom might come home hurt or not at all. But if I believe God is guiding this relationship—which I do—I need to let you be who you are and trust Him to work out the details and keep you safe."

A slow smile spread across Shiloh's face. "You mean all that?"

"With all my heart." He squeezed her hand and lightly rubbed his thumb over her fingers. "I don't know why it took me so long to realize that."

She laughed. "You only almost changed your mind three days ago."

"But I'm serious about you, Shiloh. The fact that it took me three days is crazy enough."

They shared a smile, and then Shiloh picked up her fork and went back to her Chinese food.

Repeated *I'm sorry*s, delicious food and the most romantic words she'd ever heard in her life.

Yes, indeed, the man really knew how to apologize.

Once they'd finished dinner, Adam had thought they could do something relaxing, maybe watch a movie.

He should have figured Shiloh would have eyes only for the case. She'd pulled out a legal pad and sat down on his sofa with a pen, ready to brainstorm what their next step should be.

"You haven't even seen my library yet. Didn't you say the other day you'd wanted to?" He wanted the case solved, too…but anything to distract her for just a few more minutes and keep her smiling would work for him.

The trick got her attention, as he'd known it would.

"That's right," she said, eyes gleaming as she nearly jumped from the sofa. "Books first. Then the case."

She turned to wag a finger at him as she walked down the hall—guessing correctly which way the library was. "Don't think I don't know you're just trying to distract me. I'll let you this time, but after this, it's back to work."

"It's that room on the left." The room was probably meant to be a spare bedroom, but, instead, he'd filled it with bookshelves.

She stepped inside, turned on the light and let out a low whistle.

"It's not much compared to the library…" His voice trailed off. Maybe mentioning Widow Hamilton and her unique house wasn't his best move this soon after everything that had happened.

"At the Hamilton place." Shiloh drew a breath. "I know what you were going to say. You don't have to tiptoe around me. I'll be fine."

He knew she would be. She hurt right now, but she'd learned five years ago how to cover up the pain and move on to do what needed to be done. He'd give anything to take away the load of her responsibilities, her need for justice, for just a minute and let her cry out the emotions she was keeping carefully bottled. But then she wouldn't be Shiloh.

"Besides," she continued as she stopped in front of the first bookshelf, "what you don't have in fancy shelving and centuries-old architecture, you make up for in books. I knew you loved to read and even collected some. But I didn't know you had this many." She ran her hands along the spines of a leather-bound commentary set he'd bought recently.

"I'd just started collecting books when we began dating. Remember?"

She nodded. "That's right. So you wouldn't have had this many then."

"It was actually talking with you and Annie all those times we'd hang out together that made me start taking my collection more seriously."

Shiloh nodded. "I remember. I love books because of the history behind them. Annie loved them for the insight they have into people." A smile cracked her face. "She was such a people watcher."

"A good trait for a cop."

An awkward silence fell for several beats as they both thought the unspeakable. If Annie had been watching people as closely as she should have been, she'd still be alive. Somehow, someone had gotten too big of a drop on her.

"Russians. You have Russian authors." Shiloh looked up at him with appreciation. "I'm impressed. Aren't you scholarly."

"Dostoyevsky, Tolstoy and Solzhenitsyn wrote works with some of the most stunningly clear thoughts on depravity and the human condition." He shrugged. "The pastor in me appreciates anyone who can articulate human hopelessness without Christ so clearly."

"I vaguely remember them from the college literature class I had to take. But that makes sense." She continued her perusal, nodding or making comments now and then. She had just opened her mouth to say something when she stopped cold, her entire expression taking on that look she got when she was working.

"What is it?"

"The Pilgrim's Progress." She motioned to the volume, one of the oldest books he owned, and he nodded, thinking it was odd she was so fascinated by that book. Wasn't it predictable in a pastor's library?

She blinked several times before speaking. "I don't remember seeing a copy of this in Widow Hamilton's library."

"…Okay?"

"That doesn't strike you as strange? Do you remember what she said about her Christian-literature collection? She had first editions of Jonathan Edwards's sermons, Anne Bradstreet's poetry, several of Ben Franklin's works. And countless other books we'd consider Christian classics. But no copy of *The Pilgrim's Progress?*" She shook her head. "I have a hard time believing whoever added books to that collection over the years wouldn't have made sure they had a copy of this."

"She could have kept it somewhere else. Another room where she read, a table beside her bed, maybe." Adam shrugged. "I don't think it's that big of a deal."

Her enthusiasm waned. "Perhaps. May I see it?"

"Sure."

She took the book off the shelf, ran her hands over the cover and then flipped through the pages gently, holding the book to her nose. "I love how old books smell. My point about Widow Hamilton is that someone was looking in her house for something—in the library, in particular. What if it was that book?"

"What if people broke into her house to find a book?" The question sounded more ridiculous to Adam when it was repeated.

Shiloh shot him a look of annoyance. Apparently, he was

missing something. "Didn't she say some of her favorite books were missing?"

"Shiloh, she was also about a hundred years old. She'd lose things."

She frowned. "Maybe. But books are often used as codes. They contain maps and things like that sometimes. Play along with me here for a second. Books are a piece of history that no one really gives a second glance. If Blackbeard had left a map to his treasure drawn on crinkled brown paper with a big *X* marking the spot, don't you think it would have been found by now?"

She had him there.

"But what if…" she continued, her voice rising, "he hid instructions in a book somehow? It makes just as much sense as anything else."

He hated to dampen her enthusiasm, but there was still one problem. "Even if your theory is true…either someone stole the book from her house long ago to use it to find the treasure, or it was there…"

Her shoulders drooped. "And burned in the fire." She shook her head. "It was a good try."

She returned the book to the shelf.

"It's funny that you would have reached for that one, though," Adam went on, "since it was a gift."

Her brows rose. "From who?"

And even before he said the words, understanding clicked, and Shiloh's theory suddenly sounded like the most natural thing he'd ever heard. "From your cousin…the night she was killed."

SIXTEEN

Shiloh was sure if her heart beat any harder, it would burst in her chest. She reclaimed the book from its spot on the shelf, clutching it to her chest as though if she held it too loosely, it would disappear.

"Annie gave this to you?" she asked just to make sure she wasn't hearing things.

He nodded, his face several shades paler than it had been. "The idea that I've had it this whole time and it might be the piece we've been missing…"

She saw him swallow hard.

"I didn't think anything of it, Shiloh. She came over that afternoon with the book, told me she'd found it somewhere and thought I might like to add it to my collection, that it might come in handy someday." He shook his head. "After I realized I was being called to ministry, I thought back to what she'd said and wondered if she'd seen something even then that hinted to her I might become a pastor one day. But what if…?"

"What if she'd meant it would come in handy to help solve the case?" Shiloh finally found words to speak past the lump that had formed in her throat. Still clutching the book, she sank to the floor, unable to do more than stare at it. As certainly as she knew she was breathing, Shiloh knew she held in her hands an important element of this case.

If Annie had dropped this off on her way to wherever she was going the night she had been killed, if it had been that important that it not fall into the wrong hands, then this little book might be what men had killed for.

Might be what they had searched Widow Hamilton's house for.

Could even be what they'd broken into Shiloh's house to find, speculating that maybe she had come into possession of it. That would explain why only her desk and bookshelf had seemed out of order.

Somehow—though she didn't comprehend how yet—this book was the map to the treasure.

Shiloh opened the front cover carefully. The book was in excellent shape, but it was old, and Shiloh wasn't taking any chances. The inscription was the first thing to catch her eye.

"To L—May you find reward even in the Slough of Despond. All my love—E."

She looked up to meet Adam's eyes. "*L? E?* Who are these people?"

He shrugged. "I've never even read that before. To be honest, Annie gave me the book, and I put it on the shelf."

Shiloh understood why he hadn't immediately jumped to any conclusion about the book being related to Annie's death, but he hadn't even been curious to flip through it? Maybe it was the history lover in her, always looking for a story.

"It sounds like they were in love. Or had some kind of relationship." Beyond that…

"I do know from reading the book back in college that the Slough of Despond is one of the challenges the main character faces. It's a nasty swamp he has to travel through. It basically represents the trials and discouragement that a Christian faces. Beyond that, I don't know what to tell you."

Shiloh stared at the words again, waiting for additional layers of meaning to become clear.

It was hard to read between the lines when the entire note was only one line long. She let out a sigh and frowned. "So where do we start, then? I'd hoped the inscription would give us some kind of clue, but I'm not seeing it."

"You seem to know more about books and codes than I do."

"I only know of a few options. Page numbers could be used. Certain words could be underlined.... The possibilities are endless, but hopefully, we'd be able to see something unusual. Our best way is to flip through it page by page and look for any markings that aren't original to the text itself." It was a long shot, but she couldn't think of any other way to go about this.

"Sounds good."

Shiloh turned the yellowed pages until she came to the beginning. "Would you mind grabbing that notepad from the living room, in case I need to jot anything down?"

"Not at all."

He returned within a minute with the notepad and then left again, coming back with a French press full of coffee.

She smiled appreciatively. "You're good to me."

"I want to be. Besides, this could take a long time."

Shiloh nodded, glancing at her watch and noting the afternoon was almost becoming evening. "I'll be gone before too late. Wouldn't want you to get in trouble." She smiled hesitantly, not sure if he'd appreciate the teasing.

He clenched his jaw. "It bothers me a little that they're watching me so closely, almost trying to find a place I'm messing up, but I'm attempting to be patient with them. They had a bad experience with my predecessor—I think it's made them overly cautious. Thanks for being understanding. We'll have you out by midnight anyway. I think that's a respectable curfew for two grown adults."

Shiloh went back to her work, which was turning out to be as painstaking as she'd feared. She was ten pages in. Nothing so far.

There was nothing at twenty pages, either. Or fifty. Or one hundred.

She set the book down after several hours, rubbing her eyes to stop the blurring. "It's completely blank."

"Except for all those words."

She glared.

He was quick to apologize. "Okay, I'm sorry. You're right. It's not the time for jokes."

Shiloh stared at the book where it lay next to her, closed on the floor. Had Annie truly just thought Adam should have it in his collection? Shiloh had been so sure it had significance in the case.

Certainty outweighed the doubts. She couldn't explain why, but she *knew* this book was important. She turned back to the inscription, hoping to see something there, but again nothing jumped out at her as significant.

"You don't think *E* could be Edward Teach, do you? That Blackbeard himself could have written a note in this book to someone?"

Adam's look was understandably skeptical. It *was* a stretch. But lately that described the entire case, and Shiloh figured it was better to speculate too much than not enough and risk missing something.

"That would still mean there's some kind of extra significance in what he wrote. And it seems pretty straightforward."

Shiloh nodded. She wasn't going to let this go so easily, but they'd probably done all they could for the night. Another glance at her watch told her it was just after ten.

It was earlier than she'd planned to be heading home, but for now she needed sleep.

"Let me follow you home. Especially since it's not curfew yet." Adam's eyes twinkled, taking away some of the seriousness in them. "Besides—" they dimmed again "—whoever is doing all of this is still out there. I'd feel better knowing you were home safely, in a house with only you in it." He motioned toward Tux. "Do you want to take him with you for a while, until this is solved? He's good protection."

"So is the patrol car in front of my house. And if all else fails, so is my .40 cal." Shiloh patted her purse, which she'd retrieved from the living room. "And it's a little more low maintenance than your dog." She rubbed behind Tux's ears. "Not that I don't like dogs. I love them. I'm just not home enough to take care of one."

She looked at the dog's warm brown eyes, noting how he soaked up every ounce of affection he was given, repaying it in full with open adoration, and thought she might want a dog someday after all. Her eyes flickered to Adam and then back to Tux. If things went well with their relationship this time around, maybe she'd end up with one after all.

"What are you smiling about?" Adam asked as they stepped outside, and he closed the door behind them.

"Nothing." She grinned even wider. "A lady has to have some secrets."

After Adam was satisfied that her car had remained safely locked, Shiloh climbed in and drove home, more grateful than she'd admit to see Adam's headlights behind her. He followed her home, parked his car and came in to sweep the house with her. All the rooms were empty, and Shiloh felt slightly paranoid but safe. And taken care of.

She told Adam good-night, locked the door and headed to her room. She'd just turned out the light and pulled the covers over her head when the first rumble of thunder sounded, and she felt herself tense. Not another storm. Not when she needed this sleep so much and desperately wanted to forget all the things storms made her think of.

Her cell phone rang from its place on the table beside her, its shrill ring distracting her from the growing rumbles outside her window.

Caller ID said it was the chief. She couldn't think of what he'd want this late at night, but none of the possibilities could be good. She squeezed her eyes shut as she answered, anticipating the worst, even if she wasn't sure what "the worst" would be.

"Hello?"

"Shiloh. It's good news. It's about Mary Hamilton."

She felt her stomach churn, unsure of what could possibly be good news on that front. "Okay, go ahead."

"She wasn't at her house when it caught fire. We tracked her down at her sister's residence in Macon. She's alive, Shiloh."

Shiloh let out a breath she'd been holding for days and whispered a prayer of thanks, her joy at knowing Mary hadn't died overtaking all other thoughts.

She told the chief how relieved she was, then hung up. As she set the phone down, she realized that if the book in her purse did hold answers to this case and had once been part of the Hamiltons' library collection, which was possible, then Mary Hamilton might be able to help Shiloh fit the pieces of this puzzle together.

And if Mary was alive, she'd be willing to do just that.

Shiloh rolled back over toward the table, grabbed her phone and set its alarm for 5:00 a.m. She was driving to Macon in the morning. She wanted answers, and she wanted them as soon as possible. Hopefully, Adam would go, too, but she was going either way—with or without him.

* * *

It was midmorning when Adam and Shiloh pulled into a parking space at Middle Georgia Nursing Home, a low brick building that looked as though it had seen better days.

"Widow Hamilton lives in an estate by the ocean, and her sister lives...here?"

Shiloh shrugged.

"It's kind of a dump."

"Have you ever seen a nice nursing home?" she countered.

Shiloh had point. Although he'd seen nicer than this. He had to admit, though, when they walked inside, that the place was clean and well kept. It was just...old.

Funny how time made some things—like the interior of Widow Hamilton's old house—more beautiful and made some things crumble. There was a sermon illustration in that somewhere that he could use someday.

"Hi, we're here to see Mary Hamilton. She's visiting her sister..." Shiloh's voice trailed off, and Adam realized Shiloh didn't know the woman's name.

He looked nervously at the woman manning the front desk, wondering if she'd let them in with so little information.

"Oh, sure, Mary." The woman grinned. "She's visiting with Alice right now. That's Room 12, down this hall. Just make sure you sign in on the clipboard."

Shiloh signed them in and they walked along the hall to a room where Adam could hear the distinct laughter of women over eighty.

Shiloh knocked softly, and one of them called, "Come in!"

"Good morning, ladies." Shiloh greeted each of them with a smile.

The one Adam didn't recognize—Alice—frowned.

"Do I know you?"

Shiloh shook her head. "No, ma'am. I'm a friend of Mary's."

"Why, Officer Evans. I hardly recognized you without your uniform on. Isn't she beautiful, Reverend Cole?" Mary grinned.

"She certainly is."

He was pretty sure Shiloh blushed. He liked that.

"I'm so glad you're alive," Shiloh said as she accepted the hug the older woman offered. Then Shiloh frowned. "Wait—your car was in the garage at your house. How did you get here?" Her eyes darted to Mary's sister, and Adam was sure Shiloh was thinking the same thing he was— surely Mary's sister hadn't picked her up.

Mary waved off the question with her hands as Adam and Shiloh sat down. "I took a cab, dear. It's too far to drive at my age."

Adam's eyes widened at the money that must've cost. Then again, a Hamilton, from what he'd seen of the house and estate, would have plenty to spare.

"We wanted to talk to you about pirate treasure. From the 1700s." The words came out of Shiloh's mouth in a rush. She never was one for small talk.

The widow raised her perfectly arched brows in surprise. "Treasure?"

"And the prowlers at your house. Had I told you before that I think they're connected?"

Mary appeared to consider this for a minute and then nodded. "I suppose that would make sense. I have heard my family connected to rumors of that treasure before." Sadness passed over her face. "But, dear, you know the house is gone." She softened her tone as though for Shiloh's benefit.

Shiloh nodded, emotions chasing themselves across her face too quickly for Adam to identify them. "I was there."

"How terrible, dear. Are you okay?"

Shiloh nodded.

He noted the woman's concern was for Shiloh and not for her house. Her family's home.

Mary turned her gaze to Adam. "You seem confused, young man. I'm sad about my home and all those beautiful details you won't find in another house in the South. But aren't our lives more important than our shelters?"

Her words so echoed Jesus's words in the Sermon on the Mount that conviction pierced Adam. Would he be able to keep his perspective so well in her situation? He wasn't sure, but he suspected Widow Hamilton was a remarkable woman.

Mary turned back to Shiloh. "So I'm sorry, dear, but even if the legends are true—that the Hamiltons and at least one notorious pirate were somehow connected—the house isn't there to investigate anymore. The nice man from the police department who called told me the garage and the barn are still standing, but neither of those buildings is old enough to have housed the treasure. If it was there, it's gone now."

Shiloh shook her head. "Not necessarily. But finding the actual treasure is only part of what I'm interested in. I can't explain, not now, but I need help finding where a treasure is or might have been at one point in time."

She pulled the book from the purse, which she'd kept tight against her body since they had exited the car. "Do you recognize this?"

"I believe that looks like the copy I used to have in my library." Mary reached for it and ran her hands over the hard cover. "*The Pilgrim's Progress.* It's an edition I hadn't read yet, but I used to see it up there on the shelf—until it went missing years ago." Her expression dimmed.

Shiloh laid her hand over Mary's wrinkled one. "May I see it again?" She reached out and took the book back.

"Do you have any idea what this means?" Shiloh opened to the page with the note written on it and handed the book to Mary.

Mary's eyes widened as she read. "I'd heard rumors, but I'd thought…all small towns have their rumors. Who knew this one might be true?" She shook her head. "Well, what do you know."

"So it makes sense to you." Shiloh did nothing to conceal her excitement.

"Well, certainly. It appears the note is talking about the book. Haven't you read *The Pilgrim's Progress,* young lady?"

Shiloh's face fell.

"And I certainly have my suspicions about who *L* and *E* are."

A sliver of hope found its way back to Shiloh's expression.

Mary Hamilton nodded. "Yes, I suppose *L* would be my great, great, great—to tell you the truth, I've forgotten how many *great*s there are—aunt Laura."

"What do you know about her? Anything that might help?"

"I know she died terribly young. Everyone said she died of a broken heart."

Adam felt his own heartbeat quicken. Was it possible?

"And I suspect that *E* is the man she was rumored to have fallen in love with."

"And that would be?" Shiloh leaned forward in her chair.

"Why, the most notorious pirate of them all, of course. Edward Teach, better known as Blackbeard."

SEVENTEEN

"Blackbeard?" Shiloh repeated. "Blackbeard?" She'd intentionally not mentioned the name of the pirate whose treasure she sought, not wanting to lead Mary to "remember" legends that didn't exist in an effort to help.

"Yes, dear. I'm assuming you have heard of him?"

The twinkle in Mary's eyes said she was more than aware that Shiloh knew who the pirate was. Shiloh supposed her reaction hadn't exactly been subtle.

"So your great, however many *great*s, aunt Laura supposedly fell in love with Blackbeard."

"Oh, yes." Mary nodded. "That's how the story goes. They met on accident, so I've been told, one time when his ship docked near Treasure Point. It was love at first sight. He left, of course, and went back to his life on the sea, but they supposedly exchanged hundreds of letters. Aunt Laura never married."

Shiloh felt as if she'd struck gold in every sense but literal and had the feeling even that would come soon.

She glanced back down at the book that Mary still held in her hands. Apparently, there truly was a connection between the Hamilton family and Blackbeard. But how did that get her closer to the treasure? Unless Blackbeard had hidden it on the family's property somewhere. Shiloh fought back a groan. The estate covered acres! Even if they knew for a fact that the treasure was on their land, it could still take years to recover it, if they ever did.

Mary's eyes were still fixed on the note. "You know, it also could be…" She shook her head. "No, don't listen to me. It's just the ramblings of an old lady who wishes she could help." She started to shut the book, paused and re-opened it to the inscription again. "But it's possible that…"

Shiloh waited, leaning closer to Mary.

"There's an area on the property, in the woods between the house and the ocean, that we were warned as children to avoid, due to the snakes and alligators that love to inhabit those kind of places…." Mary got a faraway look in her eye. "Of course, no generation of children listened. We all went down there to explore but found it was every bit as bad as our parents had said and never stayed long. For as long as I can remember, our family has referred to that swamp as 'the Slough of Despond.'"

Shivers of anticipation threatened to overwhelm Shiloh as her breath caught in her throat, and she reached out her hands. "May I see that again?" She motioned toward the book.

Mary nodded and delivered it to Shiloh's waiting arms.

"'May you find reward even in the Slough of Despond.' He wasn't talking figuratively. He meant it literally." Shiloh closed the book and stood. "I'm so sorry, ladies, but we have to go."

They were both nodding. "I would be upset if you did anything else, my dear." Mary pulled her into a hug. "Go find that treasure and finish this."

"I'll do my best." Shiloh had said the words so many times, out loud and to herself since her cousin's death. And finally, she felt as if she might be able to follow through with them.

* * *

"This must be it." Shiloh wrinkled her nose at the smell of decay and mud. "It matches Mary's description of the spot perfectly."

Adam, who'd waded farther into the muck than she had, took another step and the noise of the suction between his boot and the swamplike mud made her cringe.

Still, she knew if a little mud was the messiest this got, she'd be lucky. And the uneasy churning in the pit of her stomach told her that she wouldn't be. Shiloh had three goals—find the men who'd started this, make sure justice was served and keep both her and Adam alive.

The fear gnawing at her said that accomplishing all three was a lofty goal. She'd narrowly avoided death how many times in the past few weeks? Didn't that kind of luck run out eventually? Still, she didn't have a choice. They were too close to quit. She took a deep breath to push past the fear.

"Help me, Lord," she whispered as she took another step into the mud, keeping a watchful eye for gators or snakes, both of which could prove just as dangerous as the men she was pursuing. No booming voice from the sky confirmed that God was listening, but somehow confidence settled over her and she knew that He was.

"So what are we looking for, exactly?" Adam's low voice and the way he looked at her each spoke of his reliance on her abilities. If only she possessed a tenth of the assurance he did. Still, his faith in her bolstered her courage.

"That I can't tell you. The note seems to have been intended to be enough for Laura to find the treasure he'd hidden for her but be inconspicuous enough for no one else to figure it out if they found the book. He was being vague on purpose, knowing she'd know where to look."

"We could go for shovels, dig around a little," he suggested.

Shiloh eyed the area, which had to be fifty yards wide and almost as long. She racked her brain for other possibilities, places here that Blackbeard could have hidden his treasure that wouldn't require digging up the entire area. Surely if the treasure was left for a woman he was in love with, he would have made reaching it possible for her. Shiloh couldn't picture a woman of hundreds of years ago—especially one who'd been raised in as pampered an environment as Laura Hamilton—digging up the entire coastal slough with no help.

For a moment Shiloh was gripped with a panic that the treasure might have been found years ago. But the anxiety eased as quickly as it had come. Surely Mary would have known if the treasure had ever been recovered—and she'd certainly given no indication that it had. Anyway, it wasn't the treasure she needed to find; it was the treasure's hiding spot. As Shiloh and Annie had believed all along, all she needed to do was find the right location and wait. The men who had killed on their quest to find this treasure wouldn't give up until they'd found where it was hidden. And when they found it, they'd be caught.

And justice would finally be served.

Adam's voice jolted her from her thoughts. "Let's look around some more for now, make sure we're seeing everything there is to see."

With another deep breath, Shiloh waded farther in. The ground beneath her feet, under the layers of mud, was disturbingly soft, as if it might pull her in. She decided she'd start her search by walking the entire perimeter.

Shiloh was three-fourths of the way around when she stepped on a piece of ground that felt different. Harder.

"Hey, Adam!" she called. "I need your help." Her heart raced as she stomped her foot again to see if she'd imagined it. No, this place was distinctly harder. She walked a couple of steps forward. It appeared to be six, maybe seven, feet long.

Was she stomping on someone's final resting place—a grave buried along the swampy area?

"What is it?" Adam asked as he approached.

She pointed to the ground. "There's something down there," she whispered, not sure if she was afraid of being heard or trying to regain some feeling of reverence in case this was, indeed, part of a centuries-old graveyard.

"Okay. What?"

She shook her head. "Not sure. Maybe a grave? The ground under my feet here is harder. Like I'm standing on solid rock instead of mud."

"It would make sense. I was on my way over here to tell you that I saw several rock slabs that may have been headstones, over that way." He motioned with his head in the direction.

Shiloh looked down, then back up at Adam. "Do we investigate this one? Just in case? Or apologize profusely for stomping all over them and leave?" She shifted her weight and stepped off the side of the grave. As she did so, her foot caught on something. The stone beneath her other foot shifted.

She heard someone shrieking as the world tilted away and realized it was her, just as the leg she'd been standing on gave out completely and she found herself falling.

Adam grabbed for her arms, trying to get a good grip, but the ground underneath him was too slippery, and then they were both plummeting.

Smells assaulted Shiloh's nose as her body hit something hard, rolled down something—stairs?—and crumpled into a heap. The odors of the muddy bog now mingled with something musty with age. The ground beneath her was cold and hard. How had she fallen on stone? Hadn't the stone just given way?

Mud coated whatever surface they'd collapsed onto. Shiloh guessed it must have fallen into this hole with them.

"Adam?"

"Call me crazy, Shiloh, but I think we might have found something."

She loved how, despite every bone in her body aching from the fall, her mind being overwhelmed with the thought of what they were doing, her palms sweating as nerves threatened to overtake her, Adam could still make her laugh. "Yeah, I'd say so."

Wherever they were was dark, and though the hole they'd fallen through was letting in some light, it was dimmed by the tree branches above them and didn't offer much help in identifying their surroundings.

She put her hands out and felt the stone that formed the walls. "It's some kind of tunnel underground." Shiloh shivered—whether from the dampness of the space or the anticipation of what might come next, she wasn't sure. All she knew was that they were one step closer to the treasure, and they were walking right into a piece of history that had been preserved for over two hundred years.

She reached out and felt the walls again, appreciation for whoever had built them growing within her. She knew it was possible, especially with modern engineering, to build something like a tunnel under a swamp or even underwater, but the idea that someone had done it so long ago, without the technology available in the present, was impressive.

Shiloh focused and then let herself think out loud as she tried to sort through where they were. "We fell down stairs, right?"

"That's what they felt like to me."

She squinted but still could make out only dim shapes. She patted the place on her hip next to her gun where she usually kept a flashlight.

Not there. She closed her eyes. So close… "You don't have a flashlight, do you?"

She heard the same frustration she felt in his deep sigh. "No."

That left them with only a few options. And exploring the rest of this tunnel now wasn't one of them. Either they could both go back for flashlights, or one of them could, while the other stayed and kept watch here at the entrance.

"Neither of us is leaving without the other." Adam's matter-of-fact tone left no room for argument.

"Do you think we can figure out how to close it?"

"We're going to have to try. It's the only option."

Shiloh stood, keeping one arm above her to stop her head from hitting the ceiling, but when she reached up, even from a standing position, there were several inches left.

"Ouch."

Apparently, Adam hadn't put a hand over his head.

"People were obviously shorter back in the tunnel-building days."

She could barely make out his shape, but it looked as if he was having to hunch over to avoid hitting his head again. He led the way up the stone stairs, and as they walked, Shiloh finally had a moment to marvel at what they'd discovered. Secret tunnels hadn't been uncommon in the peak of the pirate days. She'd even explored several of the famous pirate tunnels in Savannah, back before they were declared a hazard and closed up for good.

She wondered if Blackbeard had specifically built this tunnel just to hide a treasure for his secret love, or if this tunnel, and others that were likely nearby, had been used to smuggle goods to and from a docked pirate ship.

Adam was almost back aboveground when Shiloh heard a noise from somewhere behind her, deep within the recesses of the earth.

She froze.

And she heard it again.

"Adam," she whispered. Then slightly louder. "Adam."

He turned and stepped back down to where she was. "What is it?" He lowered his volume to match hers.

She laid a hand on his arm. "I heard something." Shiloh felt him stiffen—and he certainly didn't relax at her next words. "We can't leave. If there's someone down there, we need to go now. Or it might be too late."

Adam felt the urgency in Shiloh's touch, heard it in her voice. What remained unspoken was that she *was* staying—with or without him. There was no way he'd get her out of this tunnel until she found what…and who… was waiting farther in. Down the stairs into the unknown pitch-blackness.

They didn't have flashlights. Exploring without them, especially when there were likely criminals somewhere in this underground maze with them, seemed foolish.

But Shiloh was right. Leaving now, knowing whoever was down there could disappear with the treasure and be gone forever, wasn't the right choice, either.

"Okay," he said.

Shiloh let out a deep breath that she must have been holding.

"But on one condition." He reached for his cell phone. "We go up long enough to call the chief for backup."

"But…" She sighed. "All right. Let's go."

They walked the last few steps to the top. Adam found the chief's number and hit Call.

Nothing happened. He glanced at the corner of his phone's screen. No service.

It figured.

"Does your phone have service?" he asked Shiloh.

She pulled it out and shook her head. "It's not uncommon in the woods around here. Especially as you get closer to the ocean and farther from town."

Adam could have hit something. Now what?

Shiloh turned pleading blue eyes on him. "Please, Adam. We have to go now. I've worked too long to let them slip through my fingers, and that's what they'll do if we leave. I know it."

He wanted to argue. But he also knew her words carried some truth.

Either decision was a bad one. But if there was a chance they could end this today and stop the threats on Shiloh's life—that would make this risk worth it.

"I've got a lighter," Adam offered. "A guy I met at seminary kept one in his pocket, and it came in handy more often than I would have thought, so I started carrying one." He slid the silver Zippo out of his pocket. "Grab a couple of branches. At least that way we'll have them if we need them and can get a little light for a minute or two. It won't be like having a flashlight, but it's better than nothing."

Shiloh waded through the mud, more eagerly than before, and found several fairly dry sticks. Adam started down the stairs, then whirled, curled one hand behind Shiloh's head and brought her toward him in a deep, desperate kiss. She returned his fervency, and Adam held her tight for another minute and then pulled back.

He summoned the courage to say the three words to her that he'd known were still true from the moment he'd seen her angry, beautiful face through his driver's-side window when he'd arrived in town.

But the focused look that came back into her eyes moments after Shiloh opened them said it still wasn't the right time. That seemed to be the story of their lives.

"Come on." She hurried down the stairs in front of him, like a woman on a mission.

He followed behind her, praying he'd get the chance to tell her how he felt and that this ordeal would have a happy ending.

Adam counted twenty steps by the time they reached level ground. They were deeper belowground than he would have expected. Thankfully, the ceiling here was tall enough for him to stand—barely.

He heard a dull noise farther in, as if something was being moved, and prayed the treasure would still be there when he and Shiloh finally found it. Or that at least the men responsible for trying to steal it from the Hamilton family, who Adam supposed it rightfully belonged to, would still be there for them to catch.

Moving around without light wasn't as difficult as he'd anticipated it would be. The tunnel was narrow, and for the most part it worked fine to keep their arms out, touching the walls slightly, to make sure they weren't missing any turnoffs they'd need to explore. Several times they'd found small rooms, no bigger than five or six square feet, off the main passageway. Neither of them could decide if they'd been originally built for storage or to allow someone to move to the side so people coming from the other direction could pass in the narrow tunnel. So far, that was all they'd discovered, though—no forks or other points in the tunnel that would have required them to make a decision.

"Uh-oh." Shiloh's whisper, though too soft for anyone elsewhere in the tunnel to hear, echoed slightly.

"What?"

He heard her arms moving around in front of him. "The tunnel is in a T shape here. There's a wall in front of me, and I can go either left or right."

Adam tried to mentally map where they'd been so far in relation to landmarks aboveground, like the house and the ocean. If they were where he thought they were, he was pretty sure right would take them even closer to the water's edge. Left would go back toward the house, which was the more logical choice for hiding a treasure. Blackbeard would have wanted it close enough to the water to make it accessible, but far enough away that high tides and hurricane storm surges wouldn't endanger it.

"Go left," he whispered to Shiloh.

"Got it." She turned and he followed.

They walked in silence, making several more turns that Adam prayed were correct. Until after one turn the muffled noises they'd been hearing grew significantly louder.

And then up ahead of them, he saw the circular yellow glow of a flashlight, its beam lighting up the dirt floor of the tunnel.

Adam's breath caught in his throat, and he pulled Shiloh along with him as he backtracked, ducking into one of the side rooms they'd discovered only minutes before. This one was narrow, maybe eighteen inches wide and about ten feet deep. Adam remembered that because they'd turned this way, thinking it was a narrow side tunnel, before they'd realized it was just another room.

He shoved her in first. Even though she kept quiet, he could feel her protest in the way she resisted slightly before giving in and seeking shelter at the end of the room. He understood that she wanted to be the one in front and in control, but he'd already vowed to keep her safe. If that meant using his body to shield her from any bullets that might fly, that was what he would do.

But for both of their sakes, and the future he hoped they'd have together, he prayed it wouldn't come to that.

EIGHTEEN

Shiloh listened to the approaching footsteps, afraid to breathe. Someone else was in the tunnel—she was sure now. She hadn't let the copy of *The Pilgrim's Progress* out of her sight, and no one would have stumbled upon the entrance in the bog by accident. Furthermore, she hadn't noticed any signs of disturbance at the muddy entrance. Most likely there was another way in—which meant there would be an additional entrance that Adam and she might reach before they were discovered.

She decided to hope that was true. Shiloh felt her arms quiver, unsure if it was adrenaline or fear invading her veins. Five years in the making and this would all be over soon.

One way or another.

She gripped Adam's arm and pulled him as close to her as possible. She rested her other hand on the handle of her Glock, the thought of possibly needing to kill a human being—which she'd never done before—chilling her to the core.

That apprehension was replaced by a burning fire once she reminded herself that these men had killed her cousin.

She listened to the man approach, the enormity of what she and Adam were tackling, just the two of them, overwhelming her as she kept her eyes glued to the floor so she could see the other man's light as he got closer. She fought to swallow but it felt as if her throat was closing. She loved being a cop, but she didn't know how to do this—capture several armed men who had managed to elude police for so many years. She wasn't strong enough.

It became harder to breathe. Her shivers increased, and she identified in a detached way that her symptoms matched those of a panic attack. It was the same way she felt whenever she heard thunder. But there was no storm outside right now, she tried to tell herself.

Panic clawed at her throat as the night her cousin had been killed flashed in her mind unbidden. Annie had wanted Shiloh to come, too. She held back a sob, knowing that to make any noise at all would give away their position and cost them their lives. Annie had had a lead and a contact whom she'd planned to meet at a well-known cemetery in Savannah where they could talk without anyone overhearing. She'd asked Shiloh to come along; Annie had said she had a feeling it had to do with the historical aspect of the case. If Shiloh heard the information firsthand, she'd be better prepared to help Annie understand how it applied to the case.

Annie had come close to begging, but Shiloh had resisted. The weather forecast had called for storms, and Shiloh had always hated them and wanted to be safe inside, not out in the middle of a cemetery.

"Just take notes," she'd told her cousin. "Tell me everything later, and I promise I'll do the best I can to help you. But I just…can't go with you."

Annie knew of Shiloh's fear of storms. Her cousin had looked straight into Shiloh's eyes and must have seen the full depth of Shiloh's terror in them, as thunder groaned and rumbled in the distance.

"Okay," Annie had finally said, hugging Shiloh close

to her. "I'll go alone. But, Shiloh, when are you going to stop being afraid?"

The footsteps grew closer, jolting Shiloh back into the present that terrified her every bit as much as being sucked into the past.

Shiloh tightened her grip on Adam's arm and fought to take a deep breath.

She should have died that night, along with her cousin. She *would* have died, but her ridiculous childlike fear of storms had saved her, had kept her alive.

She'd let fear paralyze her ever since.

Father, help me.... She struggled to pray, fought to win against the fear even as her hands shook even harder. She couldn't do it....

But God could.

A sudden calm crept over her, and her breathing slowed to normal. Truth fought through the darkness in her mind as she recalled the past and amended what she knew to be true. Her fear hadn't kept her alive. God had. All her fear, her attempts to carefully control her life to keep the fear in check...God didn't need those.

He had everything under control.

Shiloh's hands stopped shaking, and her muscles relaxed. Whatever happened, however this ended, was in God's hands.

For several blissful moments, despite the approaching footsteps and the hints of light drawing closer, Shiloh felt peace.

Adam grabbed her hand and squeezed, seeming to know without her explaining all that had happened in her heart over the past few minutes. She squeezed back, smiling at him, though she knew he couldn't see her.

Queasiness washed over Shiloh a second before the smell registered in her nose. The light was brighter now, and she focused on its proximity, willing herself not to be sick from whatever the new smell was.

Seconds passed, and as the light threatened to come close enough to give away their hiding spot, Shiloh identified the smells in her mind.

Fish and peppermint.

Understanding hit, rocking Shiloh's perceptions about this town. Harry? The fisherman she'd spent so much time talking to down at the dock? Him being here was too much of a coincidence. He had to be involved. The full implications of that made her nausea grow more intense as he drew even closer, and the light stopped.

Directly in front of their hiding place.

"I know you're there, Shiloh. You're too smart for me to have thought you wouldn't find this when we did, if not before." His raspy voice carried a hint of amusement.

She was hearing the voice of the man who'd killed her cousin. She moved slightly only to have Adam hold her back. She realized his thought as soon as he stopped her—Harry could be guessing, hoping to flush them out.

"I'm not bluffing, Shiloh. I'm trying to give you a chance to live."

To prove his point he raised the flashlight beam, slowly exposing every square inch of their hiding place and revealing his own wicked grin at having them trapped.

"You can leave. Walk right out of here and forget this ever happened. That's what my warnings to you were about."

His warnings? Shiloh thought back on the attacks against her, struggling to make sense of his words.

"He wanted to kill you—" Harry spoke again "—but I knew you could be managed without having to add your death to our list of crimes. I've always kind of liked you, Shiloh. You're spunky. Seemed a shame to kill you when we could just scare you into shutting up for good."

Shiloh knew he was serious. He would really let her walk out of here, trusting in his ability to manipulate her fear to keep him from ending up behind bars. Her stomach heaved. Behind the bravado, the uniform and the gun…what kind of coward had she been?

"The warning on your car, convincing my partner to leave the door open to warn you and not hurt you when he searched your house…I was trying to tell you to back off. For your own good. He wanted you dead and almost succeeded in making that happen a couple times, but I kept trying to warn you to get off the case—just keep you quiet without having to kill you." He smiled, as though he thought she'd appreciate the gesture.

She was supposed to believe he was on her side?

"I don't want to kill you. I will if I have to, but I'd rather not." He sighed as though her silence was too much for him to take. "So just leave and let me have the reward I've worked so hard for."

Shiloh's blood boiled in righteous indignation. Reward? He thought he deserved something, a prize, for the criminal acts he'd committed? For murdering the best friend she'd ever had?

"No." She was startled at the boldness in her own voice even as she prayed her resistance wouldn't cost Adam his life. "I'm not leaving. Not without you—and whoever else is down here—in handcuffs and ready to pay for your crimes."

Harry drew a gun, a large revolver, from a holster that sat on his hip. She wanted to scoff at his choice of firearm, outdated as this particular gun was. Who did he think he was, a modern-day pirate?

"Get out here, then." His voice had hardened. "I'm taking you to Slate for him to decide what to do with you."

Slate? Shiloh frowned as more pieces of the puzzle

clicked into place. Her old mentor—the one she'd reached out to for advice on this very case. He'd had her completely fooled.

He was likely the source who'd told Annie he had information for her. Which meant they'd been wrong all these years. Annie's death wasn't because she hadn't been observant enough. It was because she'd trusted Slate. And he'd used that to his advantage to kill her.

Shiloh wanted to weep.

"I said, get out."

Harry had raised his voice, but Adam didn't move and neither did she.

Harry cocked the hammer, and she knew he meant business. "Last chance," he warned.

She nudged Adam, who walked out of the narrow room, still apparently mindful to keep himself between Harry and Shiloh. She appreciated the gesture, but she was going to have to get him to move so she could get off a shot. As the thought crossed her mind, she angled her body to keep the Glock hidden outside of the flashlight beam, but Harry's eyes were too quick.

"Give me the gun."

She did so without resistance. First, because she knew he would shoot them both if she didn't—probably Adam first, given Harry's weird belief that he was on Shiloh's side— and second, because she had a backup in an ankle holster. It would be harder to reach, and she'd have to move almost quicker than possible to draw it and fire before Harry and Professor Slate could return fire, but it was better than nothing—if she could find an opportunity to put it to use.

"Now go." Harry kept the gun trained on Adam and hit Shiloh with his elbow. "You first." He motioned with the flashlight down the narrow tunnel. Shiloh did as he'd said and started walking.

Deeper into the darkness. Away from anyone who could help. Straight into almost certain death.

When Shiloh had handed over her weapon, Adam had felt his stomach sink. He had his boxing ability and his strength, but those were no match for men with guns.

They marched farther down the tunnel and stopped in a large central room that had several tunnels coming off of it.

In the corner was a pile of what could only be Blackbeard's treasure. Some of it was gold coins, like the one he and Shiloh had found that day on the trail. The rest of it appeared to be navigational tools. It was something out of a history book—he never would have believed it if he hadn't stared at it with his own eyes.

"Finally arrived, have you?" A tall figure rose from where he'd been kneeling in front of the treasure, dusting his hands on his slacks as he stood. "Good to see you again, Shiloh. It's been too long." The man offered an insincere smile.

"I would have thought you'd be above this, Professor Slate."

"Above taking my own place in history by finding the treasure of the most famous pirate who ever lived? Certainly not."

"Above being a criminal," she spat back.

He looked at her with a mix of pity and derision. "Any true lover of history would understand. Most would have done the same."

"I disagree." Shiloh raised her chin in defiance.

"Enough debate." He bent to pick up one of the gold coins and rubbed it between his thumb and forefinger. "Would you like to see the treasure? It seems only fair, if we're going to kill you, that you fully understand why."

The way he spoke so casually about killing them sent a

chill up Adam's spine. Something about the man was pure evil to Adam. As if he was missing his soul.

"I understand well enough. It's all part of your greed."

"Greed, ambition… Really, it's semantics, isn't it?" The man shook his head. "I'd hoped you, of all people, a fellow professor, would have understood."

She stiffened.

"Enough talking." The other man finally spoke up. "What are we going to do with them?"

Adam noted he sounded nervous, as if he was dreading the other man's answer.

"Always in such a rush, Harry."

"The longer we're down here, the better chance we have of getting caught."

The taller man gave his partner a glare that smacked of condescension. "We're not going to get caught. No thanks to you and the stunts you've pulled, like vandalizing her car—" he jerked his head toward Shiloh "—and intentionally making noise at the old lady's house to scare her."

"I thought if we bothered her enough, she'd leave town and get out of our way. Or at least be afraid enough to shut up about anything she might see," Harry whined.

Adam turned away from the man, unable to hide his disgust. What kind of person was so obsessed with manipulating people through fear?

"Which is why you're an idiot," Slate said with a smile. "Don't worry—that's why we blew up her house. To shut her up forever."

Harry blanched. "You mean…because she'd be even more scared."

Slate just stared at him.

"You said she wasn't home." Harry looked as though he'd be sick any minute.

"And you believed me? You're as gullible as you were in high school. Didn't you see her car in the garage?"

And then Harry vomited in the corner, adding to the already putrid smell that seemed to follow him around.

Adam was quiet as the men argued. Obviously they didn't know Mary Hamilton was still alive. From the sound of things, that was good, since at least Slate had wanted her dead.

He glanced over at Shiloh, whose eyes seemed to be searching the room—looking for something to use as a weapon, he would guess. Or a way to get them out of here. Adam watched as her face fell. She shook her head slightly.

"Out of ideas," she mouthed, shoulders sinking. "We need backup. I'll stall."

Adam nodded.

Slate chose that moment to turn his attention back to his prisoners.

"I suppose, idiot though he is, Harry is right this time. I'd better kill you both now so we can get out. Do you have a preference for how you die, *Officer* Evans, before I leave here with my gold and my place in history?"

"Harry's not the idiot here. You are if you really think you're going to get away with this," she shot back.

"Four bodies. I've left four bodies so far—all law-enforcement officers—and still no one has managed to find me. Either they're not trying very hard or I'm simply more intelligent than they are. The first may be true, but I'm certain the second is, so, yes. I do think I'm going to get away with this because it's true."

The man drew the largest semiautomatic handgun Adam had ever seen from a holster at his side and pointed it at them, the light from their flashlights and torches they'd lit on the treasure room's walls bouncing and glittering off the stainless steel.

"Are you ready to die, Shiloh?"

Shiloh didn't flinch. Adam saw no trace of the fear he knew had haunted her for so long.

She'd never been more beautiful to him.

Slate laughed. The hollow sound, void of any real amusement, echoed off of the cold walls.

"You're just like your cousin." Slate shook his head. "She was determined to be brave, too. Such a shame she had to die like she did."

His laughter had a harsher edge to it this time. A mocking edge. "And now it's your turn."

Slate slowly, maliciously aimed his gun and eased his thumb back on the hammer.

"Wait," Shiloh interrupted. "I still have questions."

Slate relaxed his trigger finger, raised an eyebrow but didn't lower the gun.

"You didn't explain everything." She motioned to the pile of coins. "How did Annie get a coin like that in Savannah? How did one end up in Treasure Point? And *The Pilgrim's Progress*—how did she come to have that?"

He snickered and lowered the gun slightly. "Trying to stall, Shiloh?"

"You just seemed like you wanted us to understand everything before...before you killed us." She forced out the words, not even letting her voice tremble.

He seemed to consider it. "That's true. I've never been able to stand ignorance." He sighed. "The coins were from another treasure trove of Blackbeard's that I saw on display once. It was a classy affair, only respectable historians were invited, and security wasn't tight enough to prevent two or three coins from disappearing. I used them to entice Harry—" he jerked a thumb toward his partner "—to help me search." He glared at his partner. "I suppose he must have dropped one to get your attention." Slate shook his head. "The book was lost in Savannah somewhere. Which was unfortunate, given all the research I had to do about Treasure Point simply in order to discover the book's existence and the fact that it held a key to finding the treasure. Unfortunate indeed." He glared in Harry's direction again. "And it was recovered by your cousin."

"But we found the treasure anyway." Harry mumbled. "Isn't that what matters?"

Slate ignored him. "I believe that answers all of your questions, and that's all I have to tell you." Slate raised his gun. "So if you were trying to stall until some kind of help got here, you might as well just acknowledge that no one is coming." He smirked. "You're on your own, Shiloh. And your little mission has finally, completely failed."

The shuffle of footsteps behind Adam drew Slate's eyes. For a split second, Adam saw fear dash across the professor's expression. Horror and realization that he'd lost everything in that moment raced across his face. Then his jaw firmed, he leveled his gun back at Shiloh and moved his finger toward the trigger.

"Freeze." The chief's voice boomed within the walls, and Adam swung his head to see him and three other officers with guns drawn enter the room from one of the tunnels.

Gunshots, more than one, rang out simultaneously as Adam threw himself at Shiloh to knock her out of the way.

Fire exploded through Adam's chest and something warm soaked his shirt. It was crimson red. Blood.

It was the last color he saw before he hit the floor and the world went black.

NINETEEN

Shiloh's screams echoed in her ears as Adam fell in slow motion, the bullet that had been intended for her piercing high on the left side of his chest.

Someone had taken down Professor Slate, who had collapsed backward onto the floor, part of him lying on the scattering of gold coins, which were now stained deep red from his blood. She shuddered and turned away, hating the loss of life but feeling relief sweep through her that he was gone.

Dropping to her knees, she turned her attention to Adam. "Shiloh."

His eyes blinked open and hope rose in her chest. She didn't know much about injuries like this, but his regaining consciousness so fast had to be a good sign. He'd been down for less than a minute.

"Shhh. Don't try to talk." She pressed a finger to his lips, blinking back the moisture stinging her eyes. He'd taken the bullet meant for her. The full import of that echoed in her mind and heart as a truth she'd suspected became a fact in her mind.

He still loved her.

"I love you, Shiloh," he confirmed in a steadier voice.

Shiloh bit back tears—it couldn't end like this. Not after

all their relationship had endured. "I love you, too," she whispered, knowing beyond any hint of doubt that it was true and always would be. "But please, you have to be okay."

"I will be. I kept waiting for the right time to tell you, and I realized there's never going to be a right time. Our lives are always going to be crazy, but no matter what we're going through, I always want you to know that it's true."

Their eyes locked, and Shiloh would have bent to kiss him had she not been elbowed out of the way by the same EMT who'd attended to her after she'd been shot.

The seriousness on the man's face as he did his best to treat Adam's wound in the dark, stuffy tunnel made Shiloh wring her hands and pray even harder.

The man kept working, not commenting at all. Long minutes later, Shiloh noticed the bleeding had almost entirely stopped.

The EMT let out a breath and lifted his face to meet her eyes. "We need to get him to a hospital immediately for further treatment. But he's going to be fine."

The man and several of the officers helped Adam stand and supported him as they made their way out of the tunnel. Shiloh followed, then turned back to look at the aftermath one last time.

Professor Slate was dead. The chief had cuffed a sick-looking Harry, who'd no doubt go to jail for the rest of his life. The treasure lay where it had been on the floor, soaked in blood. Shiloh shivered and turned around, vowing not to look back again.

She hurried to catch up to the men who were helping Adam. After only a few more minutes they walked up a staircase similar to the one they'd fallen down originally. It led to the middle of the pile of charred rubble that made up Widow Hamilton's old house. They were very near the spot in the house where the library would have been, and Shiloh smiled to think they'd been that close to the entrance to the tunnel and had never known it was there. Professor Slate and Harry must have found this entrance after they blew up the house.

She followed Adam to the waiting ambulance and drew in a long breath of fresh air as she soaked in the warm sunshine.

The nightmare was finally over.

After the EMTs had explained that they'd be taking Adam to a hospital in Savannah where he could receive all the treatment he might need, Shiloh had resolved to stay in Treasure Point and talk to the chief before heading to join Adam.

Her boss had waited long enough for her explanation.

He had officers taking care of Professor Slate's body and the treasure, and he told her to wait in his office until he'd arranged for Harry's transport to a state prison north of Savannah.

Shiloh hadn't been sitting for long when he came in.

"Ready to talk?" he asked as he took his chair.

She nodded. "I'm ready."

Starting at the beginning, Shiloh told him every detail she could remember, up to the point when they'd entered the cave.

"Wait." She frowned. "I couldn't call you to let you know we thought we'd found it. There was no cell service out there. So how did you know we needed backup?"

"Mary Hamilton called me and told me what she thought you were planning. Also, a couple of guys from the fire department noticed that the scene appeared to have been tampered with and asked our guys to come out and investigate. When we found the staircase to the tunnels, everything fell into place."

She nodded. "However it happened, I'm glad you came."

"You don't make it easy to have your back, Shiloh," his stern voice admonished her. "You should have told me about the case and your part in it weeks ago, as soon as all of this heated up again—if not when you came here to take this job."

"I should have," she admitted. "But when things began, I started to wonder if someone in the department was connected to the threats—especially when I mentioned here that I was going running on the coastal trail and then someone came after me there." Her voice trailed off, and she felt herself tensing. "I still don't understand how that happened."

The chief waved off her concern. "It was Hazel White."

"The secretary?"

"Apparently, she's Professor Slate's sister. Harry sang like a bird, and she's on her way to prison with him right now. It's over. You're safe, Shiloh."

The chief sighed. "You're one of the best cops I've ever seen. But this case has made it clear to me that the kind of work you're doing now isn't for you."

Her heart plummeted into her stomach, and she shifted her gaze to the floor.

"I have another idea in mind."

Shiloh looked back up at him and waited.

After days in the hospital, undergoing surgery and regaining coherency from the pain meds he'd been on, Adam was more than ready to get out and find a cabin in the woods to hide out in for the rest of his life, somewhere away from people. He didn't think he'd been alone for more than five minutes since the ordeal in the cave, between visitors and the nurses.

"Knock, knock." Shiloh smiled at him as she entered the room with two to-go cups of what he guessed was coffee. "I got it at the coffee shop downstairs, which is much better than I had expected." She held out one of the cups. "I got decaf for you, in case they're not letting you have caffeine yet."

He thanked her and took a minute to study her pretty face and those impossibly deep blue eyes.

Maybe he'd give up on the idea of being a hermit after all, unless he could convince Shiloh to come with him. Because one thing was sure—he wasn't letting her get away again.

"I've missed you," she said softly as she eased into the chair next to his bed.

He laughed, noting that his shoulder and chest hurt when he did so, but not as much as they would have even twenty-four hours ago. He was amazed at the progress he was making, and the doctors were pleased, too.

With any luck, they'd let him out of here soon, and he could get on with important things. Like dragging Shiloh to a church and finding someone to marry them.

"Any word on when they might let you out of here?" she asked between sips.

"Not too long, I don't think. They won't tell me a day yet, though." Something which frustrated him to no end. Finally, there was nothing serious standing in the way of a future for him and Shiloh, and he was stuck in a hospital bed.

If God was teaching Adam patience, he was certain he'd learned now and would be fine moving on.

Seeing how close she'd come to being killed in the line of duty had made him more uneasy than before about her continuing her job as a cop. But he'd meant what he had said about loving her for who she was. And though it bothered him, he was going to do his best to ignore it. Maybe pretend she worked at a bakery or somewhere else safe instead.

"I talked to the chief the other day. Finally told him everything."

Adam shifted to see her face better. "And? What did he say?"

She paused.

"You're in trouble, aren't you?" He winced for her sake.

Shiloh shook her head. "No. Not in trouble exactly. We did talk, though, and decided it would be best if I gave up my job as a patrol officer."

Never before had Adam's spirits plummeted and danced simultaneously. After only a heartbeat, the plummeting won out. "Shiloh, no. You're incredible at what you do. You know that. Why doesn't he know that?" He tried to sit up straighter but grimaced as the ache in his chest intensified. He lay back down, settling for strengthening his tone to make his point instead. "I'll talk to him, Shiloh. I don't know if it will help, but I'll make sure he understands how hard you worked—"

"Adam."

"—and all the things you figured out and—"

"Adam." She laid a hand on his arm. The touch got his attention, and he stopped talking and stared at her. Smiling. The woman was smiling.

"I'm quitting my job because I'm going back to school and getting some extra training. I decided—not the chief, me—that patrol work isn't where I want to be forever. I'm going to learn what I need to know to be a crime-scene investigator."

Adam blinked, sure this was a dream, and he would wake up any minute. He'd found the woman he wanted to spend the rest of his life with; she wanted so far to spend hers with him, too; *and* she was going to quit doing a job he'd never loved the idea of her doing?

He couldn't have asked for more.

"Adam?" Her voice was hesitant. "What do you think?"

"I think it's the best idea I've heard all day." He brought her free hand down to his face and brushed his lips across the back of it. "You'll be amazing at it, I'm sure."

Her entire face lit up with his praise. "I hope so."

Adam's face tightened, and he shook his head. "I also wanted to tell you that the board came to visit me earlier today, and we had a talk. I explained to them that the woman I choose to date or marry is my business, and I would be the judge of whether her faith was important to her, not them. I already told you I was wrong to let their opinions influence me. They understand now, and most of them apologized." Which was important, because Adam was excited about his future with both the church and Shiloh. It felt good to start over and move past the mistakes all of them had made in the situation.

"And, Shiloh? My dad says he's sorry, too. That as your pastor he should have been more supportive of your plans to become a cop and find Annie's killer. He says he's proud of you, that my mom would have loved you." He handed her a small envelope. "He left a note for you that says all of that, whenever you're ready to read it."

He thought he saw moisture in her eyes, but her small smile told him everything was okay. "Thanks. And thanks especially for believing in me when no one else did."

"I hope to always do that, from now on." He smiled, knowing he'd never find a better moment than right now to ask the question that had been on his mind.

Nerves gripped Adam as he felt for the ring box he'd slid under a pile of blankets earlier. His dad had visited every day since Adam had been admitted, and yesterday his dad had asked if there was anything he could get Adam from his house. This box, one of his most treasured possessions for the past five years, was the only thing he'd asked for.

His dad had teared up as he'd handed it to Adam, apologizing for putting so much pressure on him and telling him how good it was to see him happy and at peace with his choices in life. Then they'd hugged—the first hug Adam could remember receiving from his dad since he'd graduated from high school.

He took a deep breath, ready to move into the future. "I have something to tell you, too. Or to ask you, really."

Shiloh's eyes widened.

"I know it's not the most romantic place for this." He cleared his throat. "But our timing has always been atrocious, and I'm tired of waiting." He shrugged as he pulled out the box and opened it to reveal the glittering ring she'd left behind five years ago. "I love you, Shiloh Evans. I lost you once and almost lost you so many other times. I don't want to lose you again."

Tears glimmered in her eyes, making them even more blue.

He hoped tears were a good sign. "Shiloh…will you marry me?"

The tears spilled over and slid down her face.

His heart twisted. "What do you think?"

And then she smiled. "I think it's the best idea I've heard all day."

A grin spread across his face and he slid the ring back on her hand before tugging her toward him to seal their new promise with a kiss.

* * * * *

Dear Reader,

I'm so glad you joined me for Shiloh and Adam's story. When I started writing this one, all I knew was that a young woman was running from her past—that someone was trying to kill her, and she had moved to a new town with the intention of starting over. I had no idea why anyone was after her—just that she kept looking over her shoulder, waiting for her past to catch up.

At the beginning of the story, both Shiloh and Adam are controlled by fear. I am by nature a worrier, so in a way writing this story and seeing how God worked in their lives to remind them of His sovereignty helped me. It made me remember that I am supposed to give my worries to God and live without fear. That's my prayer for you, as well.

I hope you enjoyed reading this book as much as I enjoyed writing it.

I would love to hear from you. My email is sarahvarland@gmail.com, and I blog at espressoinalatteworld.blogspot.com, where I talk about life, books and living as a pastor's wife in the ministry fishbowl.

Sarah Varland

Questions for Discussion

1. How does Shiloh react when Adam walks back into her life? Do you feel you would have reacted the same way?

2. What did you think about a police officer and a pastor starting a relationship? Do opposites really attract in real life?

3. Shiloh and Adam both struggle with fear. What's something you fear in your life, and how can you work on letting go of that fear and trusting God?

4. Adam is almost swayed by the opinions of some of the men in the church in regard to his relationship with Shiloh. Are you easily influenced by the opinions of others? How can this be both good and bad?

5. Do you think you would enjoy living in a small town like Treasure Point? What would be the advantages and disadvantages?

6. Shiloh ended her relationship with Adam without telling him why. How should she have handled that situation differently? What part does communication play in your relationships?

7. People are always debating the issue of women in dangerous jobs, such as law enforcement. What are your opinions on this issue?

8. Shiloh and Adam venture into the tunnel without flashlights, knowing their actions were somewhat foolish but convinced it might be their only chance to discover the men behind the crimes. What was your reaction to their decision? What would you have done in their situation?

9. Part of Professor Slate's motivation for doing whatever it took to find the treasure was to secure his place in history. What can we do, in a positive way on a daily basis, to make sure we're remembered?

10. As a history lover, Shiloh believes that the past holds useful information for us in the present. How does knowledge of the past help you? Why is history important?

11. At the end of the story, the treasure is soaked in blood. What symbolism do you see in that?